ANNIE CHAMBERS

Lenore Carroll

WATERMARK PRESS

Watermark Press, Inc.
149 N. Broadway
Wichita, Kansas 67202

Printed in the United States of America

Cover design and Illustration by Kirsten S. Johnson

Library of Congress Cataloging-in-Publication Data

Carroll, Lenore, 1939–
    Annie Chambers : a novel / by Lenore Carroll.
        p. cm.
    ISBN 0-922820-07-4 :
    I. Title.
PS3553.A7648A84 1990
813'.54—dc20
                                                                89-39976
                                                                CIP

To my husband, Bob,
The Tuesday Night Group, and
Kathy Sherman Boutros

ANNIE
CHAMBERS

In the Life
PROLOGUE
Summer 1933

I started remembering all the things that happened to me that day when I overheard Dave Bulkley preaching a sermon over the prostitute's dead child. I don't get around too well. I'm ninety years old and I broke my hip, but I can still stand straight if I have my cane.

That day I decided to go up the back stairs to the second floor. People who come slumming like to look through my old bawdy house before they listen to my stories. I wanted to make sure all the doors were unlocked upstairs.

The window at the landing was open. I can't see much, but I could feel the dry summer breeze full of grain dust blown across Kansas, thick with pollen. I knew the window must be dirty and spotted with years of grime. I can't let it bother me because I can't afford to keep the place up any more. Once this house was the fanciest resort in Kansas City, competed with Eva Prince's, across the alley. The back windows of the two buildings nearly meet. My house is plain, but Eva Prince's is an old castle — turrets, ginger-bread, bay windows. The City Union Mission occupies it now.

I stood there at the window, feeling the heat through

my violet dress. It was expensive when I bought it at
Emery, Bird, Thayer and I had it altered to fit my tall
frame. It's old now, but good enough for everyday. I
rested my hand on the windowsill. I could feel the varnish
blistered and flaked from rain blown in during storms.
No one runs up to close the windows when it rains any
more. Once the mahogany woodwork was polished daily
by a Negro maid and the wainscoting gleamed in the
gaslight.

I heard Dave Bulkley praying. His musical voice rose
and fell in the summer heat. This was not his usual prayer
for help from the Lord; neither was this the usual time for
devotions — the middle of a Saturday afternoon. I heard
something about a child and the "sins of the fathers." I
wondered why Bulkley was praying about a child. Then I
remembered: That prostitute who lived across from the
Mission had a baby and it died. The woman wouldn't give
up the child for burial but kept the corpse in her room.
Bulkley must have agreed to do a service.

"She lived only a few months, but she planted God's
love in our hearts by her innocent sweetness."

I thought of another dead baby — my own. And the
second, stillborn. Tears rolled down my face. That happened years ago, when I was another person.

Foolish old woman! I wiped my eyes. My babes would
be old men, over sixty years old by now. Why weep over
the whore's child?

"He maketh me to lie down in green pastures . . . "
Bulkley called down the Lord's forgiveness, entreated
Divine solace. That Bulkley can pray. He is probably a
saint, to work down here in the North End with the drunks
and whores, bring his genteel wife and little girl, beg
money to keep the Mission going. Never cynical, never
bitter.

I pictured an incongruous little casket under the chandelier in Eva's ballroom, the mirrors reflecting Bulkley's
ragtag congregation.

"Thy kingdom come, Thy will be done . . . "

I tried to pray with him, but I choked on the words. I continued upstairs. There is a child buried in my cemetery plot—another whore's little girl.

I walked down the threadbare hall runner. I traced the frame on one of the heavy bedroom doors. The frames hold pictures of my girls—they were the best, the most accomplished. For a moment, I could almost see Belle taking blond Billy for his first time; see Nellie pregnant, counting towels; smell rosemary and bay and sweet thyme from Kate's room; hear the piano faintly from downstairs; hear the laughter and the groans; feel the house alive around me.

In one room I touched the foot of a brass bed and smelled old linen. I walked to the tall window. Once horse cars passed here on their way to the trolley barn across the street.

I slowly made my way back down the front stairs where brass cleats still hold the dusty carpet in place. I sat in my cane-backed wheel chair and pushed myself to my own rooms.

I can't see the gilt flaking away from the molding, the vermillion draperies and wallpaper faded to rust, the once royal blue bedspread dimmed to grey. The cloudy mirrors in carved frames send back reflections no one can see. Silver-framed images of friends and family look out, but I do not return their glances.

I slipped off my shoes and eased back onto the pillows, tired. In the old days I ran up those stairs a dozen times a night without a thought.

I wiped tears from my face again and blew my nose on a large handkerchief.

Old men by now.

Bulkley's whore took up whoring first, then lost her baby. I lost my babies first. But we both ended up in The Life.

If I could pray, I'd pray that I didn't remember so much.

But God and I have long since stopped speaking. I've lived too long. I can remember it all.

The brick facade of my house is nearly anonymous — plain red brick, two stories, no decoration. It might be a hotel, a saloon or even a respectable boarding house. On the Third Street side is a green tile pagoda roof whose edges curl upward from the concrete pillars shaped like giant bamboo trunks. A delicate lattice between the pillars shelters the doorway. Curved wrought iron railings lead up the four steps to the front door where the grimy red paint is battered and chipped.

I know every inch of the building and I am glad I cannot see how shabby it has become.

That night I ate dinner, as usual, with Murray Darling, the husband of my last housekeeper. I promised her I'd take care of him. He is my contact with the world, but unreliable. I always hated to rely on anyone, but now I must. Like the cripple and the crutch, neither of us can stand alone.

The hot, stale summer air in my room wasn't warm enough, and I felt a chill when I undressed. I took a long time to wash myself carefully from my high forehead to my sunken breasts to my private parts to my big feet with their long toes. My skin is thin and dry as chamois, faintly wrinkled like the skin on a pan of hot milk. Perhaps it is a blessing I cannot see the sagging skin, the liver marks. I rubbed glycerine lotion into my parchment skin.

I dressed carefully. When I was young, I always felt repulsed by old people who had lost that essential pride to keep themselves fresh and neat. They were usually the ones who complained about not having friends.

At nine o'clock that evening, I was ready in the entrance hall awaiting the guests. I started holding open house on weekend nights when I first tried to sell this heap. I thought it would make a good nightclub, but after the

Crash nobody seemed interested. Now it's something of a lark for young couples to come slumming in the old red light district.

I checked my chin for errant, old lady whiskers and made sure I had my handkerchief. I'll never sell this place, but the open house brings in a little money. I smoothed the black skirt and jacket, checked the lace collar of the white silk blouse to make sure it was flat, adjusted the long string of beads. I ran my hands over the simple bun at the back of my head, the only style I can manage with stiff fingers.

At last I heard footsteps and the chatter of voices, the women's high heels on the tile of the entryway and the sound of the heavy door opening and closing. The chatter died when they spotted me in the invalid's chair, so I called out, "Come in, come in! Make yourselves comfortable. Please go all over the house and look at the rooms upstairs. When you return, I'll answer your questions and tell you what it was like in the old days."

Later, when the guests gathered in the West Parlor, I asked Murray, "Are the chairs arranged?" I smelled whiskey on his breath, then the smell of cut flowers from the vases in the room.

"Miss Annie," asked a young woman, "How did you always manage to get beautiful girls?" She had noticed the photos in the frames on the doors upstairs.

"I didn't," I replied, smiling. "You should have seen some of them when they first came here. Bless you, they looked worse than homely. They were down and out. I made them attractive. I bought them fine clothes. I showed them how to do their hair. I taught them manners."

I paused to see if there were more comments. I thought of Belle and some other girls who came to my doors, then continued: "It wasn't always the most naturally beautiful girls who were the most popular. Manners and personality counted more than looks, you know."

I imagined the couples sitting on the old plush settees and standing around the heavy mahogany and walnut furniture.

"I taught them manners and charm. The men who patronized my house demanded that. They wanted their girls to be feminine at all times."

I pretended to look around, but it was the smell of cigarette smoke that cued me.

"I wouldn't allow them to smoke in the parlor," I said and laughed gently. "The men who came here wouldn't stand for it. Smoking would have given my place a bad name. It was all right if they smoked in their rooms, but never in the parlor." I smiled again so my guests would not feel scolded. "The men were finicky in those days and to have seen a girl smoke in their presence would have made her appear common."

What they did upstairs would not bear repeating to this group of naifs. What does it mean when immorality becomes quaint? Nothing improper was seen in the parlors, but everything human flesh was capable of took place upstairs.

"I taught them manners," I repeated. "They profited by my teachings, since a lot of them got husbands, fine husbands, and my girls made fine wives for them."

There was a silence until a young man's voice reached me.

"What is your, ah, feeling . . . " He searched for a tactful phrase. "About living like . . . I mean, most people think . . . "

I gave a practiced laugh. "Do you mean bringing those girls into The Life?"

There was a murmur in the room.

"Most of the girls were desperate," I said, "or they would never have come to me. And I never recruited them. Somehow they showed up. And most of them left better off than they came, if I could persuade them to save their money and look for a good man."

I'm not ashamed of anything I did in this business, but people think I should be.

"I got them husbands even after they had come to my place believing that they were ruined forever. After a while they began to have hopes, and no girl who has hopes wants to stop in a place of this type forever, no matter how well it is run and how congenial the surroundings," I said.

Only I have stayed here forever.

"Fine men, prosperous men came to my place. I taught the girls how to act. I kept them from boozing. I encouraged them to think of getting married. I've gotten hundreds of letters from my girls after they were happily married to good men, men who married them right out of this house where they became acquainted with them. I can't show you any of the letters, because I always tore them up.

"Almost none of those girls went back to the old Life. But lots of them came back to visit me here. I've had lots of friends in my life. Why just look at all these flowers." I gestured around the room to the vases I knew Murray had placed there.

"Last week was my birthday. You should have seen the flowers. Most of these came from the south side of town, too."

The questions continued. I only told them about what went on downstairs. Let them imagine the rest. It must be strange for them to see an old woman, grandmotherly but bright, and think of her as a Vice Queen. Besides, the wages of sin should be death, not healthy old age.

I dropped my handkerchief when I adjusted my jet beads and there was a flutter until I found it. Then I began my life stories in a voice loud enough for all to hear. They had been improved in the telling, with the painful parts left out.

After that day I kept thinking about all that had happened to me, trying to see if any of it meant anything.

People always wonder how a woman ends up in The Life. Perhaps if they knew my story, they would learn. Something about that day—hearing Dave Bulkley preach, telling my stories to the guests, shook loose the memories. They came tumbling around me like walnuts in a cold wind, reminding me of who I had been and how I became what I am.

Summer 1859

It has been over seventy years and I still remember that dress, that day, as though it had just happened. The blank clay of memory took clearer impressions when it was fresh.

Abraham Lincoln was candidate for president in 1859, and some of the girls in Sullivan wanted me to ride in a parade they were staging for him. We made up the yellow riding habits in secret—they had black trimmings at the bottom. And when the big day arrived I stole my mother's saddle from the house and was in the parade. It went right by my father's hotel and there he stood on the corner watching me.

When I returned home he said I had disgraced him. You never heard a girl get such a going over as I got. He was from Kentucky and against Lincoln.

I suppose if I hadn't sewn that dress, taken the saddle and ridden in the parade, everything would have been different. Little things happen that lead to other things and your life is set in a new direction before you realize it.

I enjoyed making the riding habit at the house of a friend. We girls got together to sew and talk and giggle. The yellow jacket had a round, flat collar with a black cravat. The ruffled skirt was very full and long. We didn't have top hats or boots, but we thought we were something. I was tallest so I rode last in line.

That day we looked like huge yellow roses bobbing on their stems with one drooping petal where our trains fluttered down the horses' sides. The summer sun blazed down through the yellow ruffles, almost transparent in the light.

We sang along with the little band the Republicans had gotten together—two cornets, a banjo and a drum—as they marched down the main street ahead of us, stirring up excitement. The carriages of the older women and men followed us to the stand that had been built under some big walnut trees by Hack Trudeau's general store. I remember we dismounted and sat on the ground on both sides of the stand while the speeches went on. People visited and shouted back at the speakers. The men tilted a jug and the women talked and kept an eye on their children. Some of the girls in yellow flirted with fellows taking a day from farming. I didn't listen to the candidates. I was looking over the crowd to see who looked at me. Sweat gleamed on the men's tanned faces. Horses switched flies with nervous tails and the women fanned themselves with the same gestures.

The crowd trampled the walnuts underfoot; the wagon wheels tore their soft green jackets and broke the thick black shells. From time to time one fell from the trees and made a loud plop on the wooden stand or a softer thud on the ground or the roof of a rig. The black-bark branches gave out thin twigs which bore the leaves. Each twig's leaves cast a spiral shadow like a ghost daisy. The nuts were already heavy on the branches, weighing them low toward the ground. Walnuts leaf out late in May and don't bear every year, then they begin to drop their leaves early, in September. Sometimes there is only a pile of thin twigs and dried leaves from the tree. But that year the crop looked promising and the nuts heavy and ready to fall. We brown-stained the backs of our yellow skirts with crushed walnut shells, sitting on the ground as we did. Nothing much grows under a walnut tree, just blue and white violets, or maybe some creeping, bell-flowered pennyroyal. It is as though a walnut tree wants to keep other plants away, killing anything it doesn't like, out of defense for its own ground or itself. It takes a week for walnut stains to clear away from your hands. It never came out of the skirt.

I don't remember anything about the speakers because I was so full of myself that day. After the speeches were over, we paraded back down the main street of Sullivan and accompanied the candidates one mile out of town. Summer birds sang beside the road as we stirred up the dust and the day's heat warmed the cicada's buzz. It was too far to the railroad, where the candidate would take a coach to the next town. I could blame it all on the Jefferson, Madison and Indianapolis Railroad, if blaming did any good. The railroad was too far away, They never built the spur to Sullivan; that's why my father had bought the hotel. If the hotel hadn't been such a burden on my father's mind, he wouldn't have been so harsh with me.

"Young lady! Come here!" my father shouted. I dropped my hat and gloves on the kitchen table and started to put my mother's saddle back on its peg outside the door, but he shouted, "Come here!" again. His voice was so loud and angry that I dropped the saddle on the kitchen floor and hurried to his office at the front of the building. The office was always dark and shuttered against the sun, dark-paneled wainscot and heavy wooden desk and cupboard. He never opened it up to the light. I could smell whiskey on his breath over the dusty smell of papers from the rolltop desk.

"What is the meaning of this?" he shouted. Perhaps not just those words, but some like them so full of anger they made me cringe back out the door. The force of his voice was strong as a push. I couldn't answer. What did he mean?

"Why do you do this to me?" he bellowed. "You appear publicly with that man, lead his carriage. You make me foolish in this town." He started coughing and had to stop his rant. So that was what it was about. I'd forgotten or ignored or chosen to disremember that he was a Democrat. I had been afraid he was mad because I'd taken the saddle without asking. Or because I'd spent the money on the yellow lady's cloth for the riding habit. How bad could it be, I wondered, to dress up and ride through the town looking pretty and smiling and singing? It was just a lark.

When my father stopped choking I walked over to him and knelt on the floor in front of his chair and put my hands on his knee.

"Don't be mad, Papa. I just wanted some fun."

"This isn't fun!" He grabbed my shoulders so hard it hurt. "Displaying yourself like a hussy for the whole town. I haven't raised you to be a witless strumpet."

He shook me by the shoulders until my head bobbed and my teeth snapped, then he jerked his hands away as though he were afraid he'd hurt me. I fell back awkwardly on my heels. My hair was coming loose from the pins. I honestly hadn't thought it was important. I knew my father could talk endlessly about politics, but I didn't think it was important enough to make anybody, much less my papa, teeth-rattling mad.

"We all thought it would be a jolly picnic," I said lamely.

He looked at me with sadness now his anger was spent.

"I'm disappointed in you, Leannah."

I decided to press my point, since the weight of the row had shifted to me. "What cause do you have to be disappointed in me? I didn't do anything wrong, not what you're talking about."

The fire blazed in his eyes again and he dragged me to my feet. He hadn't spanked me in years, not since I was a little girl stealing sugar lumps out of the jar and leaving the pasture gate open. I was afraid he was going to strike me, his hands gripped so hard.

"No sass from you, lady. While you live in this house, you'll do as I say."

"You never said anything about riding in a parade. Am I going to have to read your mind?" I shouted back.

He raised his hand to strike me, then stopped.

"You don't do *anything* without my permission!" The veins raised up in his temples, his face flushed and all the tendons and ligaments in his neck stood out like rigging on a sail. "As long as you're under my roof."

"Then maybe I'd better not stay under your roof!" I knew as soon as I said it that it was a mistake. I wanted to suck the words back into my mouth and swallow them, but it was too late.

"Fine. Very well, missy. You leave. And where do you think you'll go?"

"I don't care. I'll find someplace where people are reasonable." I wanted to weep and say, "No, Papa, I'm sorry," but it was too late.

My mother came into the office and saw us bristling at each other like a pair of feisty dogs. I don't know how much she had heard.

"What's going on?" she asked and that just started us up again. We said more of the same and louder and she tried to act the referee, but the more we shouted at each other, the stubborner my father got. Finally, I said I'd go stay with my Aunt Hannah and her husband, H.E., at Mount Vernon.

"Go then, and go to the devil," shouted my papa and stomped out of the room. A look from my mother warned me to keep silent, but I was ready to go to the devil or anyplace else, so long as it was away from Sullivan and my father.

Hannah was mama's sister who lived in this little town in Indiana, a day's ride from Sullivan. When I got older I came to understand that my mama was a smarter woman than I gave her credit for when I was young. She must have known the fight wasn't just about riding in a parade, but it was about the railroad, and the empty hotel and the fact that I was eighteen, old enough to be a strumpet, if I chose to be, and that papa couldn't swallow those ideas.

I liked Aunt Hannah and her husband, who had a farm just outside Mount Vernon. I had visited there when I was little and picked sour cherries from low-branched trees and gone fishing in the creek with my skirts tucked up.

"You pack up your things in that little chest under my bed," Mama said, "and tomorrow I'll get someone to drive you to Mount Vernon."

I felt as though mama was trying to get rid of me and my heart broke to think that neither parent cared about me. I began to cry and mama stopped in her calculating. She wrapped her arms around me, though I was taller by half a head.

"Here, now, what's the matter?" she murmured and stroked my back.

"Nobody wants me," I blurted, all tears and running snot. She wiped my face with her handkerchief.

"No, no," she crooned. "That's not it. You're getting older now and you need to try your wings. Besides, you're too much like your papa — hot-headed. Stay with Hannah for a while and everything'll cool off."

"What am I going to do there?"

"Oh, Hannah will think of something. Now you wash your pretty face and take off that dress and get the trunk packed while I write a letter for you to take." She gave me a pat on the rump like she used to do when I was little and I went to pack feeling a little better.

I finished my education in the town where I lived with my mother's sister's family. And it was a good education, too. I taught school in that town for a year, then decided to go home to Sullivan to see my mother. I'll be blessed if they didn't elect me school teacher there.

I think I always knew how a whore feels. In those days a woman was helpless, a nothing unless she was married. All her security, her position, all her money depended on a father or husband. Without their protection, she had no place in the world. A young woman, certifiably virginal, could keep school, as I did. Or sew or do laundry. Or hire out to work for a family in domestic service. In the cities, a woman might work for a dressmaker. A woman could own a store, but not work in one, except in lingerie. Nursing was not yet respectable. Homesteading out West was a faraway possibility. There was marriage or the life of a spinster, as part of another woman's household, dependent.

One night a master of construction for the Louisville & Nashville railroad stopped at the little hotel for the night. He was on an inspection tour and a problem with a bridge or somesuch had delayed him, so he decided to sup and sleep in Sullivan.

Willie Chambers from Lexington hit it off right away with my father. He was nearly forty; he seemed as old as my father, with a broad forehead and thick mustaches and sideburns. He was not pretty, but he seemed the very essence of dependability and authority. A heavy gold chain hung across the buttons of his waistcoat and a black broadcloth coat covered burly shoulders. He smelled of bay rum and cigars and always praised my mother's cooking lavishly.

He made up to me, but I wasn't interested.

Willie was friendly, warm and funny without overstepping the limits of propriety. After the first visit, he somehow needed to stop over in Sullivan every few weeks. Mama insisted I remain in the parlor after dinner to be with the men, but every time I tried to join the conversation papa would scowl or interrupt me. Mostly I listened and fetched drinks. All they talked about was politics.

Willie looked as though he'd like me to join in. I read

the same papers as they did and had my own opinions about Lincoln and the War. And probably more sense about it, but nobody was interested then in what I had to say.

One night, after Willie had been courting me and talking to my father for months, he waited until papa left the room. Then he turned to me and clumsily took my hands.

"Marry me, Leannah."

I tried to pull away, but he had my hands. I looked all around, trying not to look in his eyes.

"I love you and want to make you my wife," he said.

He was saying all the right things, but nothing was happening inside me. He leaned over and kissed me on the cheek, his mustaches brushing softly. I thought my heart should pound and my knees go weak, but it was just old Willie. I squeezed his hands and laughed.

"Come along, now. Don't tease." I pulled away and moved across the room. He followed me like the faithful man he was.

"Not teasing."

Now I did have to look at him and I saw in his eyes all the love any woman could ask for. It was plain he loved me and somehow I felt it was mean not to say Yes and let him have what he wanted so badly.

I didn't know what I wanted. I didn't think it was this. I had seen enough to know love wasn't like romantic books, but I thought there was a life of possibilities and I didn't want to settle for the first man who asked me, no matter how nice he was. I didn't know then I'd never get what I wanted or that I'd get things I hadn't thought of.

Papa liked him, Mama liked him. I liked him, but I wasn't in love with him. Marrying Willie would always leave me wondering what I had missed.

"Marry Willie," said Papa.
"No," I replied.
"Why not?"

"He's too old."

"Old enough to be a man and do his job," said Papa.

"He's going bald."

"That's not important."

"He's just not exciting."

"You don't want an exciting husband—that kind brings too much grief."

I didn't reply. I was 20, practically a spinster and a schoolteaching spinster, at that.

"You ain't getting any younger," mama reminded me. She could count, too.

I think they wore me down. I don't remember ever saying Yea, Nay or Maybe. Willie sparked me with little gifts and chat and never ceased begging me to marry him. All through that winter during the War, he asked and asked. I finally agreed to serve out my contract to the school board and marry him in the summer. It took a lot of worry off my mind. I would have a husband and a position. My life would be safe and familiar. We would even live back in Lexington. I would be mistress of my own house.

Mama and I filled the traveling chest with trousseau lingerie and gowns. Evenings I sewed on ribbon ties and rosettes and fitted lace insertions in the handkerchief linen camisoles.

"Sew a ruffle around the bottom of your nightgowns," my mama advised. "They'll end up around your neck, anyway."

She tried to get me ready in every way. When I think of her, I think of those evenings we sat and sewed and talked woman to woman, not just mother to child. We fussed over a cream silk peignoir, to get it to hang properly, and made lots of plain drawers and corset covers for everyday.

We made my wedding dress. I have a picture of us on our wedding day. Willie is trying not to grin, but you can see canary feathers in the corners of his mouth. I'm trying to look agreeable. I think I was beautiful then, but my stern expression makes me plain. I could never smile at the camera. The snug silk jacket of green and blue plaid taffeta fit my full, high bosom and the skirts whispered over the hoops and petticoats. This was before the fashion of white for brides, with all the symbolism loaded on after.

We spent our wedding night in my own bed in Sullivan, after celebrating. The whole town, I think, spread dinner on plank tables outside the hotel and the cider poured freely. My pupils from school eyed me shyly and wished me good-by. The men drank too much and Willie and I went upstairs at sundown to much catcalling and whistling. Willie loved me probably more than any man ever did after, but he was clumsy as a virgin moose that first night. I didn't know any better. He finished while I was still wondering what he was doing and he fell asleep while I lay there, wishing I could go back to the party, wondering if this was what everyone thought was so wonderful. There were other nights when the party was downstairs and I was upstairs wondering what I was doing.

I think what you don't know can't hurt you and you can't miss what you've never experienced. If I had known what loving could be like, I'd have felt cheated. As it was, I took it in stride. Being married meant freedom from my father's house although I went from his to Willie's with only the time in Mount Vernon for my own.

In Lexington I kept house and took care of Willie, who doted on me although I could never make myself more than fond of him. I was there in his bed at night when he began his maneuvers and I tried to be cooperative. I looked at the wallpaper over his shoulder and gripped the brass head of the bed and listened to the song of the springs. We both got sweaty and it was nice to be touched and we laughed and made the kind of private jokes married folks never tell anyone else. I couldn't complain, but there was no excitement.

It was a little like turning a trick, I learned later. I lay there and faked it and sort of enjoyed it and went along with it. It wasn't bad; it just wasn't much of a muchness.

I was pregnant by October.

Willie Chambers almost made me human. He was patient and loving with a willful young wife. He took care that I had good help in the house and that I had plenty of books to read and company to keep me from being bored when he traveled. He almost wore away the shell I had grown around me after my fight with papa.

The first time you're pregnant is probably the most self-centered time in your life. You are as filled with your self-importance as with the child. You catalog every pain and twinge, aware from minute to minute of what is inside. You are carrier, home, nourisher, goddess, defender. Your body is no longer yours, but his. When the time comes, it seems as though you both are ready to separate, but cutting the cord doesn't cut the bond. Each time he cries, the milk rises to the nipples. His cry commands.

When little Willie was born, the shell got worn away entirely.

At first I didn't know what to do with a squalling, puking baby. I nursed him and took care of him and after a while we both got used to his being out in the world. At first I was so tired and melancholy I didn't think I could keep him, but that passed. Soon, he knew me and looked toward my voice when I entered the room. He turned his face toward anything soft, searching for my breast. He smiled and cried and looked at me. Babies look at you better than anybody. Even a lover, or a husband. Nobody looks straight in your eyes with so much interest as a baby does. Willie's eyes were blue, of course, and big, like babies' eyes always seem. We could just sit, after he'd nursed, and look at each other for a long time before he got restless. He was the most beautiful thing in the world to me.

I stroked his head where gold hairs just barely showed,

fine as feathers, and watched the throbbing of the pulse in the soft spot. Sometimes the sunlight was behind his head when I held him and it made a shining halo of his fine gold baby hair. His blue eyes were so blue that even the whites seemed blue. His lips were moist and pink, his nose just a nubbin. He started to walk early and lost some of the soft baby fat. He staggered at first, his arms held out for balance, but nothing would keep him down. He must crawl and creep and walk; he must eat and soil and cry. He must look and taste and smell. Nothing could stop his push to learn everything. I looked to the day when I could teach him his letters and numbers.

When he was that little we went to the back garden, with its fence to protect us. I sat on the grass and watched him toddle, now tasting a flower, now putting his lips to a leaf. It was so hot and his dress was in the way, so I took it off and his napkin. His pink skin glowed in the sunlight and he crowed with the pleasure of freedom. When he fell he felt the soft grass with his bare knees and palms. He rolled in the grass and laughed. I laughed, too, to see him so happy. I took off my shoes and stockings so I could share the damp, soft grass with him. He chased a butterfly and I got to my feet and hurried after him. The butterfly escaped, but I picked him up and felt his sun-warm baby skin with my arms. I swung him around and around in the sun until we both were dizzy, then we staggered on the grass. I lay on my back and he fell on top of me, then climbed up and lay with his head on my breast and the sun shone through his golden hair.

Maybe if I hadn't gotten pregnant again so soon, maybe if Willie Senior had left me alone or maybe if I hadn't been so ripe, it would have been different. The new baby inside dried up my milk and I couldn't nurse the one I had.

When he sickened, I was a crazy woman. We tried everything the doctor said, everything Old Mrs. Manning suggested. I almost went to the black witcher woman, but I feared God would punish me if I did. Every day he grew thinner. The flux grew worse—more than you would have thought so small a body could hold. He shriveled up until he looked like a changeling—an old man, thin and pot-bellied and grey. At first he cried, cried day and night until I thought I would go mad. I would run in a frenzy down the street to escape his cries. Then the crying stopped altogether and he lay still and silent and then he was gone. I wanted to die myself. I wept for days. I looked for the laudanum bottle, but Willie had gotten rid of it. After nearly a week when I did not speak and barely ate, Willie strode into the bedroom.

Without a word, he whipped the bedclothes back and pulled me up. I hung back, complaining. His eyes were red from weeping, too, but he was stronger than I and more patient.

"Get up, Leannah," he said in his soft Kentucky drawl. "You don't want to lose the one you're carrying, too."

That stopped me. I hadn't been thinking about the little chipmunk inside. I reluctantly got up. Willie filled the tub in the kitchen and helped me off with my stale clothes. He washed me as gently as I had washed our baby and afterward he dried me. He was more used to wiping down a horse than a woman. Then he combed my hair until it was dry, then pulled a fistful of ribbons from his pocket, selected one and tied my hair back. He handed me a dress and we went to the dining room for dinner. I didn't eat much, but I did eat. He opened a bottle of wine and I wanted to drink the whole bottle, anything to go back to sleep and forget for a while. It made me half sick to drink a single glass. Then he sat me down in the parlor where the afternoon sun poured in on the Turkey carpet.

"We must go on, Leannah."

I did not reply.

"This is bad, but it's a burden we must bear."

I had heard enough about bearing burdens at the funeral.

"It won't be the same! My baby is dead. I want to die, too. There's no reason to keep trying if they're going to be taken away."

"What else is there to do but keep going?" Willie sat beside me and took one hand in his. "We made another baby. Think about it. That's the best thing to do. You'll see, it'll be good again."

And we went back to the bedroom. He petted me and held me and let me cry some, then we made love for the first time since the funeral.

I've since read that germs cause disease, but nobody in Kentucky in 1864 knew much about germs. They talked about milk sickness. Babies died every summer and no one knew why. What germs caused what disease? People still don't know. Fewer babies die, nowadays. But the whore's baby died and she mourned as any mother would.

Willie, because he was a good man and because he loved me more than I could ever love him, decided that Lexington wasn't healthy. The War went on in other places, and the railroads were always vulnerable and he was gone for weeks at a time. So he sent me back to Sullivan where I'd be with my mother and the rest of my family, where I'd be safe and looked after. He even instructed my brother, Dick, who worked in the livery stable, to take me for a buggy ride every day for my health. The fresh air was good and it got me out of the house. I liked Dick. He was big and blond and I felt reassured because he was strong and quiet. He couldn't read books, but he could read horses.

I remember that ride. Dick and I sat on the seat of the trap in companionable silence as the horses clip-clopped down the rutted country road where old trees met overhead. The buggy creaked and rattled along in the growing dusk to the steady beat of the horse's feet. The trees were just beginning to show green tips. In the shadows the thick brush and weeds in the ditches gave back their damp smell. The birds were ending their evening calls and it seemed as though the whole world was getting ready for sleep. I leaned against Dick and rested my hands on my big belly under my cloak.

We rode out of the woods toward cleared fields and a redwinged blackbird darted out of the brush in the ditch. The horses shied and reared; I nearly fell backward out of the rig. Dick hollered, "Whoa, whoa," and hauled on the reins with his strong hands. The horses neighed, their graceful necks strained and taut, their delicate legs thrashing, panic in their rolling eyes. They raced down the wheel ruts out of control. Dick pulled back with all his strength, shouted, "Stop, whoa, damn you!" I was too scared to make a sound as I tumbled around the seat. Then one of the wheels hit something and I flew out of the rig, soared for a brief moment, then hit the side of the ditch. My head snapped against a stump, then blackness, blackness, waves of bloody redness, then nothing.

They carried me home unconscious and the child was born dead. It would have been another boy. They told me I was in a coma three days and when I woke up, I learned papa had lost the hotel. I couldn't take it all in. There was too much pain. Then they told me Willie Chambers had been killed in a fall from a trestle where he had been supervising construction. I took his wedding ring from his cold, stiff hand.

Gradually, all the bad news sank in and I was left as hollow as a walnut shell when the good parts inside are gone.

My position, my security was crushed like that shell under a wagon wheel. I was alone, widowed and childless. I began to feel the shock of my misfortunes. Nights of no sleep and worries and pain, and worse—self-pity that was more destructive than all the rest. My misfortunes had come so fast and all together that I began to wonder what was the use of struggling against my fate. Before all that happened I had received letters from girl friends who had gone to Indianapolis and entered places of ill fame there. For all that I had been a proper school teacher, I knew what they were doing. Country girls are no strangers to coupling. The wages in the shops weren't enough to live on. They wrote to me and told me everything that happened.

Maybe that's what put me on to the idea.

Dear Leannah:

Don't tell my mama, but I quit working for that Mrs. Crenshawver in her millinery. My new address is at the bottom of the letter. Mrs. C. was the awfullest thing! She told my mama that she would look out for me, pay good wages and give me mercantile experience. Well, she kept us all in a hot, dingy attic room upstairs over her shop. We ate oatmeal every day and meat maybe once a week and never had any privacy. She took half the $4 a week she paid us for board and believe me, it took the other half just to buy the necessities!!

One day a woman wearing the elegantest shot silk dress came in with two younger women, also very well turned out, and I waited on them. The older woman told me if I wanted different work to come and see her. The other girls at Crenshawver's told me she kept a "resort." Well, I had a big fight with the old biddy Crenshawver and told her she was a cheat and mean when she held back some wages because I came in late one night.

I went to the "House of Ill Repute" and talked to the madam. She told me I didn't know what I was getting into (and I didn't!!) but I was dead set on it. I drank some whiskey the first night and now I've got so I'm used to it. (The whiskey and the work.) Sometimes it seems like fun, with singing and joking and the fine dinners, and I even like the rest of it, sometimes.

I made 14 dollars the first night! That's more in one night than I made in three and one-half weeks at the shop! And I didn't have to spend 10 hours a day on my feet to do it. I sent mama a nice present at Christmas and I'm putting money aside for when I get married.

Now, don't laugh, Leannah, but I have a boy friend and I met him at the house. He was in for a lark and liked me and came back. He's got mining interests in Idaho and when he's ready to leave, we're getting married and I'm going West.

I'm telling you because you wouldn't tattle and you'd understand, or try to. You were the smart one. Remember the day of the Lincoln parade and our yellow dresses? Those were the good times.

Hugs and XXXXXX-

"Poppy"

I believed that everything and everyone, even God, was against me. I decided to go to the city and have a short life but a fast and merry one.

A destitute woman in those days had little choice. Make another marriage (but that was difficult with most of the men away in the War or dead), or find a school board that would accept a widow. At the very least, a woman could become a domestic servant, some housewife's slave from dawn until the rest of the household slept, working day and night at the whim of the employer, subject to indignities of spirit and fighting off advances from male members of the household.

People who have never had to face total destitution prefer to believe that no woman chooses prostitution. They have created the myth of white slavery and blamed drugs and alcohol to explain the presence of women in bordellos. A woman without resources could choose to work 20 hours a day to earn a subsistence wage as a servant or spend a few hours every night on her back to make many times more. No woman made the choice easily, but many made it freely.

After settling all my bills in Sullivan I went to Indianapolis. At the train station I took a hack and directed the driver to take me to "the best resort in town." He gave me a look I cannot describe—I still smile to think of it, him staring at my widow's weeds as I asked him to take me to the whorehouse.

Once The Life was a refuge for diseased drabs, but about the time I entered, the Grandes Horizontales of England and France changed that. They were cultivated and smart. They could judge horseflesh, manage their fortunes, and be as clean and well turned-out as Milord's maiden aunt. Cleanliness had much to do with their success, I believe. Milord needn't fear disease, so he was as safe with his mistress as with his wife.

I honestly can't remember my own first night or the first week. I have seen hundreds of girls survive that first night. It is never easy. Perhaps Mrs. Chevalier, my first madam, told me the same things I always told my girls. I never encouraged them; I never had to.

When a girl knocked at my door I told her everything bad. I described the dangers of disease and the hard life she would have to live and kept asking if she still wanted to stay. In practice, I made my girls skin them back and scrub them good before they'd accept the john. It was good business to protect ourselves and if by some chance a girl contracted a dose of the clap, there was the mercury cure, which was worse than the disease and usually left the woman barren. The Life is no harder than many another and a sight easier than domestic service, which many girls were trying to escape.

Mrs. C. asked me where I was from and advised me to change my name and that first night I became Annie. My papa had called me Annie when I was little. I was ever a willful child. "A word from me and you do as you please, Annie," he used to say. Annie for Leannah and Chambers because Willie had no family for me to worry about and I didn't want to bring shame to mine. Chambers, private rooms, I liked that. And then, it *was* my legal surname.

Up till then I had been a good woman, but I was punished as though I was a sinner, so I decided to become one. Maybe it all happened because there was some evil in me and I would have done something bad if the babies and Willie had lived. I decided I didn't believe in a God who killed babies, who let men fight wars, who destroyed families. Poor old God. I blamed Him for a lot. He failed me, so I denied Him.

Even if I could have found a teaching position where they would hire a widow, I couldn't stand to spend my days with other people's children tearing at my heart. I refused to become a servant.

If I couldn't have the love of my own children and of my lawful husband, I'd find another kind of love—carnal and thoughtless. Lewd solace, I thought then. I knew I had to do something to make sure I was alive.

Other women faced worse hardships and didn't go into The Life. They were poor but respectable. What did I care for "respectable" now? It wouldn't pay the bills. I couldn't have cared less about morals. I couldn't believe I could be more unhappy than I was already. I thought it would be short, but I am nearly ninety and seventy years in The Life. They were fast, the years, but only sometimes merry. I was ready to be damned and thought I could set my foot on the primrose path in the parlor of Mrs. Chevalier's resort. The melancholy eats inside some people. I was that way after my first baby died. But after all my disasters I was too agitated to sit by the fire and weep. I had to get out, go somewhere else, do something, anything.

I had to start building the shell again, this time thicker and tougher, with more layers than a walnut shell. I've held a hundred babies, some born in this very house. It got so it didn't make me cry every time and I could laugh and enjoy them, but it never quit hurting entirely. I could even weep for the dead child of Bulkley's preaching.

Old women don't talk honestly about sex. I'm tempted not to, either. When they are no longer interesting, they lose interest. Old women with a dozen children forget who they were and how they acted. They turn to religion and become prudish. Maybe it's easier than remembering the way they really were when they can't be that young and sex-besotted anymore. I can't pretend sex wasn't important: it was my business. Still, it is painful to remember a firm neck, the chain of Venus faintly etched. The arms and belly and thighs rounded and firm. The skin smooth, unscarred, not dry as chamois. Everything moist, all the secret places ready to pour sweet wetness. To stand straight-backed without hurting, to have joints limber and never aching. Teeth strong in a mouth ready for eating. To see clearly again.

Perhaps prudery is right; otherwise it is too difficult to remember those days of quickening blood and emotions.

When I tell people that I fell "desperately in love," they seem to know what it means. It is a convention of romantic storytelling, a short way of saying something no one seems to know how to describe, once the time is past.

When I remember that time, I remember that "desperately" meant without hope. I wanted to live my life in a haze of brandy and drugs and sex, live it out as fast as I could, fling it away. I despaired. No man to love me; no babies to love. No position as a wife or daughter or even a poor widow woman.

My nights had a hectic gaiety.

I was the tallest woman in the house (although Mrs. C. surpassed me in girth) and the one who drank the most and laughed loudest and oftenest. I took drunks and learned to handle them. I took the crazy johns, who wanted extras. I learned to crack a bullwhip without breaking the lamps and to please the ones who wanted ropes or chains or other props. I learned to spot the ones who liked to hurt women and gave them a quick exit. Chevalier never questioned my judgment. I managed the house when she was laid up with pleurisy, ordered meals and found laundresses and bossed the maids. Laundresses were always a problem because of all the linen a first-class house had to use.

After a few hours when I slept as though dead, any slight noise awakened me, I woke every morning when the sky beyond my curtains first became light. I lay abed reading until the rest of the house roused. I read the *Harper's Weekly* and *Harper's Bazaar*, *Godey's Ladies' Book*. I bought the biggest books I could find on the dullest subjects, hoping they would put me back to sleep, but they almost never did. Following that plan, I educated myself haphazardly in philosophy, sometimes economics, the workings of government, which led naturally to history, so I could learn what politics had been before my time. Theology could put me to sleepmore often than anything, and I still could not find out the importance of the differences that separated the Protestant sects. After all, they all seemed to be praying to the same God. Except for the Catholics and the Jews and the Quakers, there wasn't a pennysworth of difference among them. But then I was a practicing pagan and my mind lacks the subtlety necessary to enjoy that kind of thing.

I read the *North American Review* and bought new novels and histories as they came out. I went to Mrs. Chevalier's Finishing School and learned a thing or two besides the regular curriculum.

When I tell people that my "only real love affair" began in the bawdy house in Indianapolis, it sounds like something from a pulp novel. But they seem to understand what I mean.

I walked in a half-crazy 23-year-old widow and left an experienced whore. One of my customers began visiting nightly and I fell "desperately" in love with him. It was another step in The Life.

Autumn 1865

When I think of the next part it seems to have happened to someone else, but I remember and I don't let an old lady's lies make it something sentimental and pretty.

I remember it was a night he slept over. Even though I kept a whore's late hours I still woke early, unable to sleep, edgy and tired. I went over to my big dresser. In that house there were only rooms—you turned tricks and lived in the same room. Later I tried to offer my girls a choice so that they could keep the two separate, but they usually chose to have their own rooms.

I stood naked and flatfooted, tall for a woman and I was full-fleshed then, though not as much as I finally was before I began to shrink into this old woman's body. And I lifted the brandy bottle and drank from it, tipping it with a practiced gesture and drinking the burning liquid in thirsty gulps. I can't believe I once drank that much or that way, but I did. I smoked opium, injected cocaine, drank laudanum, sniffed ether. It was all legal then, of course. Anything that would take the pain of remembering for a while. I could do those things and still look decent and turn tricks when I was twenty-three.

Standing at the dresser, honey-colored hair dragging down my back. Smelling of sex and sweat and last night's brandy. Even before pulling the chamber pot from under the bed, I drank.

"How long are you going to keep that up?" he said from the bed. I remember those words as clearly as though he were saying them right now, clearer than a phonograph record. I jumped and looked over to the bed. I hadn't realized he was awake when I slipped from beneath the sheets.

"Keep what up?" I said and poured some brandy into a glass, ladylike.

"The drinking, Annie."

"Just a little, to get started," I said, trying to keep my voice light. I couldn't look him in the eye just then, so I pulled a wrapper from the scarred cherry wardrobe and started back to the bed. The morning light grew stronger and I could see clearly the cramped room with its heavy, mis-matched bed and dresser. Coal oil lamps with dirty chimneys sat on low tables on either side of the high bed, their wicks turned down, casting a dim yellow glow over the linen and the doilies under them.

I stared at him in the morning light, stared at his shoulders and chest with its tickling hairs. I knew the rest of his body, hidden by the sheet. We were a right pair of contrasts—me big, full-bosomed and fair; him bigger, lean-muscled, shoulders broad as an ax handle, black hair almost blue in some lights. I remember his body as well as I remember his voice. I memorized it, as I memorized poems when I was a child, and with childhood's memory I can recall his young body word for word, line for line. He is indelible. I always remember the things I couldn't have and keep trying to get them in my reveries and dreams. Sometimes I still waken from a dream of him and I weep and rejoice.

"Don't you think you've done your dramatic routine long enough?"

I was so mad and hurt I threw the glass at him. The brandy flew out in amber swirls and he caught the glass.

"You go to hell."

"You're the one on that path," he answered. "How long have you been in this house?"

"I don't know. Six months, a year. So what?"

"A year of decadent posturing is enough."

"Posturing! You don't know what I've been through!" My throat knotted, choked on anger. "I lost everything — my babies, my husband."

"You should have crawled in the coffin with him. It would have been faster and easier than trying to kill yourself with liquor, but then you wouldn't have an audience."

"You think this is an act?" I whirled, then went at him with fingernails. "I'll show you."

He grabbed me by the wrists and I tried, but I couldn't hurt him. My anger became hot tears that washed my face. I tried to scratch him, knee him, anything. Hurt him back for daring to say those things. He got his leg between my legs and forced me on my back. It was a wonder we didn't wreck the bed or draw someone with the noise. I raked his arm with my nails, broke one so that my finger bled. He held me fast and every effort I made to hurt him he answered with strength. Each time our bodies clashed, I slowed until we moved together in synchrony as we always did, whether fighting or making love. We ended up with the mattress coming off the creaking springs.

Willie Chambers had been a good man, but he didn't know much about pleasuring women. Richmond knew everything. When he started buying the night, I liked him well enough. He was gently spoken and good mannered, even in a bawdy house. Then, after he satisfied himself, he turned to me, teaching me what my body would do. At first, in a brandy and laudanum haze, I watched his efforts from somewhere far away. But eventually I became more addicted to him than to any drug.

By the time we finished that morning my tears had dried.

"Why do you hurt me?" I asked.

"To shock you. To make you think. You are too fine to live like this."

"You're not too fine to visit me here. Nearly every night," I shot back.

"I love you," he said. That made me cry again. Since Willie died, no one had said that so I believed it.

I tried to substitute sex for love but Richmond saw through my cynicism. I wanted nothing better than to be loved and cared for, but it is easy to say, "I love you," and difficult to do anything about it.

"You're going to stop drinking," he said.

"I can't stop and work here."

"Why don't you leave here, Annie? And when I'm able to arrange matters, we'll get married."

For another month he came nightly and begged me to leave with him. I wanted to be with him, to leave the house. I didn't know what "matters" were in the way of our marriage. I didn't want to hurt anymore, and I craved his affection, so I risked it. After months of aimless insecurity, he offered me something to hold on to. I would have a position again, however tawdry—I would be his mistress.

I had no money of my own saved. I got $2.50 a trick, half the price, but it was spent on books and brandy, lingerie and laudanum. At last he persuaded me and I moved to a hotel where I continued to see him daily. He cared enough for me to shock me and argue with me, enough to support me, cosset me, treat me like a lover. I had thought our attachment would be only carnal.

When he said he wanted to marry me, Richmond lifted me up with a breath and held me in the palm of his hand. I felt as though I could fly. When he came to my rooms, we made love and I did fly.

He was a businessman, wealthy since the war, and an

elected official of the City of Indianapolis. Sometimes he visited me in that hotel suite early in the evening. We would bed and he would be off to a meeting or something. Sometimes he would come late and stay the night, leaving directly for one of his offices in the morning. He owned a foundry near the railroad tracks where they made iron parts for railroad carriages. I never understood exactly how the business worked except that they forged the parts for machines on orders from other fabricators. He was called there from my rooms one night and I rode in his carriage. It seemed the depths of Hades — the smell of the fire and coke and metal, the sparks flying up in the dark sky, the glow from the lamps and fires.

I listened when he talked, tried to understand what it was that made his business interesting for him. He'd started the company with borrowed money as the war started and while he had no government contracts, the demand for his products increased. The war was over, Lincoln dead. Grant was president and everyone settled into the changes.

When Richmond talked I'd suggest ways of dealing with people. Sometimes he tried what I suggested; sometimes it helped. I told him that if he respected his workers, he should listen to them. He took to wandering through the foundry and sometimes sitting with the laborers over their dinner pails. His businessmen friends thought he was lowering himself, but he found out better ways of doing things, promoted the good workers and raised their wages. His business prospered.

He was also an alderman on the Indianapolis city board. People seemed to think if a man could make a success of one thing, he'd be successful in another. Richmond didn't expand the boundaries of democracy, but he made useful contacts and one hand washed the other.

I was used to filling my time with books and brandy. I couldn't drink one or sit still with the other, so I became a champion walker. I walked from my hotel at the heart of town to the country outside and back, taking a biscuit or apple for lunch. I walked for hours through the rolling country. When I went walking I favored a riding habit. The close-fitting jacket was becoming and the dark fabric set off my coloring and fair hair. The skirts, which looped over starched white petticoats, were flirtatious but proper. I tied a low-crown hat with a length of gauze and strode on my way.

I walked so I couldn't drink and so I couldn't count the hours until Richmond came. Quit the alcohol, left behind the morphia which is so easy to find in The Life and so scarce outside it. I dropped it all with scarcely a ripple of unease. Walking sweated out the booze and made me strong. The muscles under the woman fat firmed and I felt better than I had since I was a child.

My true addiction was Richmond. It was as though I had given up all small vices for one large one. I believe, although it may only be my fancy, that you can become addicted to a person and suffer physical withdrawal pains as well as mentally yearn for his presence. Not just a beating heart as when a girl thinks of her lover, but gut-doubling spasms of loss and pain.

Making love with Richmond was like falling into a deep well. There was darkness surrounding us, no matter what time of day, no matter what light. We often made love in the late afternoon, lying on the springy brass bed in the hotel room as the winter sunset shone through the high-corniced windows, through the lace curtains which broke the light into a thousand pieces on the bare, wide-planked floor.

Sometimes the light was dim when it rained or when overcast made the light grey and cold. Then I would light the lamps early, anything to banish the shadows.

But still it was like drowning, plunging downward into icy water. Or perhaps I was the well into which he plunged.

He would come to me when his offices closed. I was

always dressed and tried to order dinner, but he had no thought for food. He complained about my clothes, but I knew that to greet him *en dishabille* would remind us both too much of where we had begun.

Sometimes in his haste, he would take me standing, only afterward subsiding into the deep featherbed and quilts. After making love, Richmond liked to smoke and stare into the fire. I put off my disarranged dress and pulled on a cashmere sacque of sky blue. The dressing gown collar was cut like a geisha's kimono so that my neck was revealed. The sacque was soft and warm and it slowly took on the smell of the two of us: my cologne, his tobacco, our rut. That combination even now of lavender and burnt Latakia makes my breath stop.

"I can't keep doing this, Annie," he said one afternoon, his lips burried in my neck, whispering kisses into my hair.

"Doing what?"

"Rushing over here. One day, I'll have my clothes off in the carriage."

I stroked his broad shoulders and squirmed because kissing my neck made goosebumps.

I never knew what part of my body he would attack with his frenzied lovemaking. It seemed as though my whole body was ready to respond and wherever he began was the right place.

One day he began at my knees. I had never even noticed my knees. They aren't the most attractive part of the body. His fingers recited their scars from childhood disasters. He played with the loose puppy skin. I stroked his head, the handiest thing to reach when someone is at your knees. I twined his hair around my fingers and stroked and scratched as though he were a cat. I had already begun to feel the loosening and moistening that his touch made when he took a gentle finger and ran it over the tender flesh behind the knee. It was a shock.

When he heard me gasp, Richmond rolled me over and kissed that place where the blood rushes close to the surface in blue streams. I wondered if I would orgasm from just those kisses as the warmth welled in my body and the familiar tension built.

At last, he ran his mouth with fluttering kisses up my thighs and found the secret place. He pushed me down into the well. I fell, then darkness closed in and it was only me and him and our bodies locked, seeking relief over and over.

I exploded at the bottom of the well and dizzying waves swept over me, then he entered me, his plunge. I wondered if he hurtled into the same oblivion or if he needed some different image for his swift collision and release.

Then we lay motionless, spent. Sometimes we were breathing heavily like racehorses after a run; sometimes we were still as corpses. Sometimes I blacked out completely. Once or twice I peed in the bed, the climax past all control. One time I knocked him off me onto the floor and only his laughter brought me back. I thought I might drown in that well into which I plunged so eagerly, but each time I would open my eyes and swallow with a dry mouth and look around to find myself back in the world.

I moved from the hotel to a house I rented near the outskirts of town. Richmond was generous. I filled the house with curve-leg chairs and cherry tables and big, stiff settees. Two friends, who had been in The Life before I arrived in Indianapolis, came in with me. I tried to be a madam, played at it to keep busy during the long hours I was alone. Richmond didn't encourage me, but he went along with the idea since I didn't turn tricks. I tried to remember Mrs. Chevalier's routine, skimmed over the rest.

The wedding kept being postponed and I grew bored, once the house was furnished. I still walked daily and wondered as I walked why I was not more dissatisfied. I was content to dwell in limbo. I hadn't gotten pregnant; perhaps I could not. The trees changed colors after a steaming summer and still I walked and waited.

When I found out, when I could no longer pretend I didn't know, I remember waiting for him, warming myself on my rage. When I am mad, I cry and I didn't want to cry that day or lose my temper. I stood in the middle of the room. Styles had changed and there was no longer a circle of crinolines surrounding me. I wanted distance that day, but hoops had got pulled back in bustles.

Sometimes I can't remember dates, but I can remember a dress I wore or something that happened or a trip I took and that is how I date things. This was the second winter after I came to Indianapolis and I cannot forget.

Richmond strode into the parlor where I waited, threw his coat and gloves on the table and came to grasp me with hands still cold from outdoors. I stood rigid and did not give him a welcoming embrace. He immediately dropped his arms and backed away. I couldn't breathe in that thick silence. He did not speak, even to ask what was wrong. Afternoon sun hid behind thick clouds and the day seemed darker than it was.

At last I said, "Is there already a Mrs. Richmond Phipps?" I did not weep nor rail nor shout, but spoke in a hollow voice that frightened even me.

He started to speak, raised his hands in supplication, then nodded and dropped his hands. I wanted denial, pleading, begging, explanation. But he was silent.

"That child, that little boy I saw last week in your office. Is he yours?"

Again he nodded.

"Why?" I could hear whining in my voice and stopped. Then the pent rage overflowed. "You've lied to me and led me on and kept me. Bastard! These 'matters' can't be taken care of. You have never told me you were married, nor mentioned divorce." The word made him flinch.

"Your business would survive, but the scandal would keep you from being re-elected to the city board."

He nodded.

"You know how much I depend on you, how much you mean to me! Why, *why* did you do it?" Anger and hurt and betrayal came flooding out in a storm of tears, but I wouldn't collapse into his arms.

"How could you, damn you, how could you do it?"

I shook with anger, as though I'd taken a chill, teeth almost chattering. "Why did you do it?"

He stood motionless, contained, balanced on some invisible point. He raised his hands and held them a foot apart, chest high, then slowly he spread his arms out to me.

"I love you."

That was all he said. My heart grew soft in my breast and I wanted to leap into those arms, but instead I screamed, "Is that all you can say, you bastard?" Then I lost all control. I shook; I screamed; I thrashed at him. "You've lied to me for a year, you son of a bitch! You've taken advantage of me. You've lied about marrying me. You even have a child. A wife you go to when you leave me. Liar! Liar!" I choked on my rage; a coughing spell stopped me. When that passed, I waited, but all he said was: "I love you."

That fired me up again and I asked him: "Does love destroy what it loves? Does love make promises it can't keep? Does love live in lies and deceit and more lies?" I began stalking back and forth in the parlor, kicking my hems out of the way each time I turned in my path. "Is this what you call love — all talk and smiles covering corruption underneath. Hypocrite!"

"I love you," was all he said.

Finally, I sat on the chair by the fire too exhausted to do anything but shudder and weep. He stood in front of me, the fire turning one side of his dark face crimson.

"What else could I do? I shouldn't have taken you from

the house, kept you as my mistress, put you here at all.
Much less do it in spite of my responsibilities. What else
could I do? I loved you too much. I should've been honest,
left my wife, left this city and gone away with you. But I'm
a coward. And selfish. I didn't want to give up any of it.
Other men do it, so I thought I could, too."

I couldn't look in his face. I knew I couldn't look in his
eyes.

"I didn't know . . . " His voice trailed off.

"Know what?"

"This passion." He stopped and tried again. "That it
could rule me. I can't marry you and I can't give you up. I
love you."

I had to wipe my eyes and blow my nose. I could not
stop weeping. I stood and wrapped my arms around him
and we stood at truce that way. I remember his hands,
usually warmed in a moment, still felt cold on my back
and the fire warmed one side of me.

"I love you," I whispered.

"Yes."

At last he pulled away from me. "Let us marry each
other here, alone, before God with no encumbrance of law
or religion." A smile began on his face. He pulled me by
one hand and we stood, side by side in front of the leaping
flames of the fire and prayed to its gods to recognize our
union.

"I, Richmond, take thee, Annie, in lust and fire and
love."

"I, Annie, take thee, Richmond, to the fire of my
heart."

We kissed delicately as though we were beginning
lovers.

When I took the ring off Willie Chambers' cold hand, I
had slipped it on my middle finger. Whenever I looked at
my left hand, there was my own ring on the third finger
with Willie's beside it. I pulled Willie's ring off and put it
on Richmond's right hand. We began again that afternoon

and in tenderness and affection rebuilt the ways we loved each other.

We continued another season, another year. One day I was walking in Richmond's neighborhood. I knew the area and often walked past his house. I had seen the woman before and the children and wondered what their lives were like.

The woman motioned me over and called me by name. I stopped and went to the gate where she stood with three children clustered around her.

"I know of your affair with my husband," she said. "I beg you, give him up. I know I could win him back to me and my children if you would help."

She actually did say those words, like someone in a melodrama. Perhaps she thought that was how a Woman Wronged should speak.

I wanted to fight, to scream, to deny. But there was something about the small, dark woman and the children, all dark as Indians, except for a towheaded baby. The little girl in a stained pinafore tugged at the woman's skirts, but Mrs. Phipps ignored her. The woman's grey morning dress billowed around her and the older boy sensed something was happening and tried to lead the little girl away, but she hung on, rumpling the fine cambric. The baby in the woman's arms rested his fair head on her thin shoulder.

"Are you really married to him?" I asked stupidly.

She pulled a ring off. She had wrapped a ribbon through it to keep it on her delicate finger.

"Is this yours?" she asked.

I looked inside and engraved there was my own name. "How did you . . . ?"

"He took it off one day and put it on his dresser. I picked it up and kept it. He knew I had it, but I refused to give it back."

"He told me he lost it."

I promised her I would leave him.

When I saw the little boy in Mrs. Phipps' arms that day with his head on her shoulder, a strand of her hair had come loose from the braids that wrapped her head and he brushed it against his cheek as he sucked his thumb. The sun shone through his blond hair, fine as feathers, fair as down. His hair with the sunshine on it halo'd his head.

It reminded me of the days of happiness before I lost my own babe, days of sunshine warming his pink skin, shining through his fair hair. Why couldn't this woman be happy with these children, leave Richmond to me? I stood in dumb silence and stared at the sun through the little boy's hair.

"I know I could win him back," she had said, "if you would help."

Why should I help her ruin my life? Did she think she could learn some pillow trick that would make a difference? Did she think if I just disappeared it would save her marriage?

When she handed me the ring and I knew it was Willie's wedding band, I felt a pain as though someone had reached inside my breast and tried to squeeze my heart dry.

"He told me he lost it," I repeated.

I watched tears well in her eyes and roll down her sallow cheeks. The baby absorbed her feelings and began a whining, fussy cry that she tried to hush with a steady pat on his back.

It sounded like melodrama. It felt like tragedy. But I wanted to laugh, as though it were a comedy. When I tell people that is what she said, they nod and accept it as though people really spoke that way seventy years ago. Perhaps Mrs. Phipps thought these were the words she was supposed to use when confronting me. Perhaps she didn't know her own banality, but it made me want to laugh. I knew if any of the laughter escaped, it would turn hysterical and overwhelm me. This was the end I had refused to see — that there would be no divorce, that Richmond and I would never run away together, that this woman and her children were real and not to be ignored. Then the hand that squeezed my heart dry pulled itself out and brought my heart with it. There was just an empty thing that pumped blood, with no spirit left.

I nodded and hurried away with Willie's ring in my hand.

That night Richmond came to my house. The other girls were out and the housekeeper was gone. I waited in the parlor. I dreaded to hear his horses outside and I went to the door and waited, then let him in.

He took me in his arms, but knew at once that something was wrong. He took off his coat and gloves and waited.

I felt rooted to the floor. I clenched Willie's ring in my pocket. I didn't want to say anything. I did not want to say what I had to say.

"We're through. I'll not see you again."

I can't remember the exact words, but I remember they were as banal as Mrs. Phipps'. I don't know how I managed to say them.

"What is this?" he snapped.

"I talked to your wife today. She showed me this." I flung the ring at him. It hit his chest, bounced off his waistcoat and fell to the floor. It rolled under a chair and I could see it catch the fire's light.

"What has my wife done to you?"

"Nothing. But she convinced me that you and I are at a dead end."

"Never."

"She thinks if I leave, you'll be faithful to her."

Richmond walked to where I stood. I brushed away from him and went to stand in the middle of the parlor.

"She gave me the ring—Willie's ring—that we pledged with. How could you be so crass? I gave you everything I could give and you let it slip away. You hypocrite! You want everything. You want your little wife waiting at home, keeping your house in order, bearing your children, making your life comfortable. And you want me here, for your pleasure."

"Yes. I want you. I've always wanted you, howsoever I could get you. I was already married when we met. What was I supposed to do? Leave them? Leave you? I wanted everything. I still do."

He stood with his knees flexed and his fists clenched, as though ready to take on a brawler.

"And where does that leave me? I'm your mistress. I have no status, no claims. I can only wait here in the shadows until you come. I can never have a family, never have children. I'm the other, and they must come first."

"What else can I do?" The question might have sounded like weakness, but for the anger in his voice.

"Kiss me good-bye. Leave me alone."

"I won't let you push me away," he gritted.

"I'm not pushing you. I'm already at arm's length. I'm telling you we're quit." I walked over to the settee by the fire and sat down. I was ready to burst into tears, or scream, or claw at him. I tried to take a deep breath.

"I can ruin myself," I said reasonably. "I already have. I don't want to ruin you. I won't take you from your wife."

He started toward me, but I got up from where I sat. I had to move away from him, out of arm's reach. I couldn't think when he touched me.

"Why are you doing this?" he asked, also reasonably. "You'll make both of us unhappy."

He was right. Why was I making us both unhappy? Then I thought of the frail, dark woman surrounded by children, standing at the gate. I should be the woman with Richmond's children, in his house, with him. I should be the woman with the worries. I should wear the crumpled morning dress, feel the girl's hand grip my skirts. I should be the woman who saw to Richmond's shirt buttons, who wondered what to have for Sunday dinner, whether to get the little girl new frocks. I should hold the child, warm on my bosom, whose hair shown golden in the sun.

I would make us unhappy for that golden child.

"I promised your wife I'd leave you."

"That doesn't mean you have to," he countered.

"Yes, it does."

"She need never know."

"She knew more than you thought."

Richmond was silent. He paced back and forth in front of the fire. "We'll be more discreet."

"That would not be satisfactory."

"I can't leave you."

I didn't know what to say. When he said that, the tears began. I hiccoughed and the words came out through my sniffling nose.

"I love you," I said. "If I didn't love you, I wouldn't care about all this. If I stay here you'll never be the man you could be to your wife, to your children. I don't want to make you do things that make you less than you are."

"You're being sentimental," he spat. He had stopped with his back to me to listen, now he turned on me, like a fighter with a second wind. "That's mighty fine talk for a whore."

"That's mighty low talk from a city father and prominent manufacturer."

"I'll never let you go free." His voice was thick and raw as a bloodied fist. He thrust his face into mine and I could see bits of spittle at the corners of his mouth.

I backed away, but I would not lean away. His breath came in short bursts and I thought he would bring down the house like some mad Samson. He grabbed my arm and I tried to twist away, but he held me fast. He knew I was right and that made him even madder.

"Do you remember, before I left Mrs. Chevalier's, what you said? You told me some cold truths I didn't want to hear. I listened. Now you listen: You hurt your family because every minute you give me is a minute they don't have."

He pulled me to him and I could feel his short breaths on my face.

"I won't leave."

"If you won't leave me alone, I'll go away."

"I won't let you."

"You can't keep me."

I caught a glance of us in the mirror over the mantle. We looked like a pair of tired fighters, winded and red-faced, but not ready to quit. I didn't know how much longer I could contend with him. My patience snapped.

"If you loved me, you'd let me go," I screamed in his face. My throat was raw as a fresh cut.

"By what distorted reasoning have you come to that?"

"I'm living half a life." I coughed and tried to stop crying. "My life is barren. I have no friends, except through you. I can never be seen in public with you. I'm a prisoner." I stopped him with that.

"How will you live without me?"

"I'll run this place as a first class bordello."

"The Devil take you! I'll not allow it." He became hard and tough. "You can separate us, but you won't humiliate me." His mind raced ahead of mine. "Everything's in my name here. If that became known, I'd be ruined."

"I'll be discreet." The mockery in my statement made him lower his head between bunched shoulders.

"I'll take care of you, madam."

He flung my hand away and turned toward the door. I thought that was the end of it and sagged into a small straight chair. I hadn't wanted to end with bitterness, but bitter or not, it must end. I searched my pockets for another handkerchief.

Then I felt his hand clamp my shoulder. He pulled me into his arms and buried his mouth in my throat. I felt the quickening and loosening. I was always ready to receive him and he knew it. In anger, and in love, he took me standing, one last time. It was quick and brutal, yet I found that darkness, that swift collision and release.

In a few moments I sank back into the little chair. He said nothing until he stood at the door with his coat on. I sat up straight and braced myself.

"I'll take care of you, madam," he said and left.

I remember crying all night.

I can say I was "desperately in love" and "I cried all night," and sound as stolid as a walnut tree in winter. I was not stolid that night. I wept until my face hurt and then I stopped. I poured brandy into a tumbler. I had not had any alcohol since I left Mrs. Chevalier's. The brandy burned a path down my raw throat. It made me sick, sicker than I was already. I ran for the kitchen and threw up in a dishpan. I had to wash my face. I changed into nightdress. I had to think about what I would do, now that Richmond would no longer take care of me. I hadn't worked it out. Would he be petty? What did he mean when he said he'd take care of me? Would he have me thrown out of this house? Take away the furniture, the clothes and jewelry? He knew powerful men; he was a powerful man.

I cried again and pulled on a heavy wrapper. I went to sit in the parlor by the fire. I saw the glimmer of the ring and picked it up from under the settee. The room was quiet, but I was a cyclone inside. Ideas scattered like walnuts in a windstorm, ideas of revenge and hate. Of publicly calling him down. Of suing him for breach of promise. I could run away, go to Chicago or St. Louis. I could beg him to forget and take me back.

The fire died and I grew cold. I got up and went to bed. I lay there, running what we had said through my mind. "I'll run this place as a bordello," I had said. So I would. If I couldn't have a normal life, with a husband who loved me and children, then I would be the least normal kind of woman there was. I'd go back to The Life and I would embrace it. I could run this house; it made enough money to keep me going. More girls, perhaps. I could go back to whoring, if it came to that.

I woke up when I heard the housekeeper stir up the fire for breakfast. I washed and dressed and went about the day as though nothing had changed. I held on to the routine of daily actions, to keep steady. That way I could get from one hour to the next. Habit was a line and as long as I didn't let go, I wouldn't be swept away. I said nothing to the girls that night, but prepared for business as usual.

About midnight, the third day after Richmond's last visit, things were going as usual. The three girls were in their rooms with customers and I sat in the parlor chatting with several men who had finished or were waiting. I jumped at the heavy pounding on the door.

"Are you Annie Chambers?" asked a rough-dressed man.

"Yes. What do you want?" I stood in the door and barred his way.

"I have a warrant to close this place as a disorderly house." He pushed his way past me. "All of you, get out." The customers hurried for their coats. He stormed through the house, pounded on doors and repeated his demands. The johns left in a hurry, stuffing their cravats in their pockets.

"On whose orders have you come?" I said as he stomped toward the door. He gave me the name of the police chief, who I knew was a friend of Richmond's. So that's how he would take care of me.

The girls came out of their rooms and clustered around me.

"What are we going to do?"

"Why did they come tonight?"

"Are we going to be put in jail?"

I asked for tea and we all sat in the dining room. I told them Richmond and I were no longer friends.

"He'll make it impossible for me to stay in Indianapolis.

I'll close this place and leave. I'm disgusted with Indiana-polis, anyway," I said. They began to murmur. "You just came back from Kansas City, didn't you, Tess?"

She nodded. I remembered all she had told us about the city.

"Well, let's go there," I said. We talked it over that night and only Tess agreed to go with me. We sold all my furniture and were ready to leave by the end of that week.

I wanted to rant and weep, beg Richmond to take me back. I wanted to kill him, burn his house and assassinate his wife — that weak, ignorant woman who had pushed me to do what I had done.

I hated and loved him. I raged and argued with myself and with the phantom Richmond in my head. I deplored his pettiness — how dare he close me down! I had provided a second establishment for his convenience. It was small of him.

But I could think of small, mean revenges I wanted on him. I could scandalize him by appearing in his office and making a public scene. I could waylay him in some public meeting and cry him for a whoremonger. I could torment his wife with his infidelities.

I did none of these things. I comforted myself that, for once and probably the last time, I had done something virtuous. Cold comfort.

Instead, I wrote a letter. It took many drafts before it was done.

"Dear Richmond:

Here is the lease.
I'm keeping the jewelry. I've sold the furniture.
I'm leaving Indianapolis and will never seek contact with you again.
I do this from love.

— Annie"

There were a thousand things I wanted to say, but I couldn't find the words.

Tess and I went to a fine hotel in Kansas City and lived there until she became insulted at a remark directed at her by one of the men we met. It was wide open in Kansas City and plenty raw. I decided to open my own house. I had met a few prosperous men and thought I could make a go of it. I rented a house down on the levee and I remember the date — 1869 — because that was the year the Hannibal Bridge opened. The city changed because of the trains that would roll over that bridge.

I can still remember the Fourth of July that year. Brass bands blared. People in their summer best trickled down toward the river to a bunting-draped bandstand erected near the bridge. Every space on lawns and streets and porches was covered by sweating people, palm leaf fans at the ready. Politicians and speculators were heroes for the day and everyone applauded their words. That evening fireworks exploded over the glassy river. Everyone shouted and waved flags.

I decided Kansas City was a pretty good place to stay.

One day not long after that Fourth of July, one of the prosperous men I knew came to my resort on the levee and said: "Annie, why don't you leave this section and move up town? All you've got here is a hurrah house."

I thought his advice was sound and in 1871 I moved up here to Third and Wyandotte. There was a little cottage here then and I rented it for $30 a month. I had three or four girls. But as soon as the owner learned the kind of place I was running he boosted the rent to $50 a month. Later, I decided to take the cottage next door and build a hallway connecting the two. This ran my rent up to $100 a month.

These prosperous men liked the hospitality of my resort. I couldn't have done what I did without friends. While I drew some men from Quality Hill's proper houses, others came from the plains, their pockets full of money from buffalo hunts and cattle drives, mining operations and property transactions. Ft. Leavenworth with its officers and scouts was only thirty miles up the Missouri River.

In 1870 the city's population was officially 32,268. I know that for a fact this was inflated because city fathers needed a population over 30,000 to issue bonds. It was probably between 20,000 and 25,000 with a large transient population moving through the city on the way west. Independence had been the place to start on the Oregon, California and Santa Fe trails, and Kansas City and St. Joseph were popular jumping off places. The railroads converged in Kansas City and carried westering families, men looking for their fortunes and all the ragtag population looking west to the future.

There was no regular police force until '75 and the laws against gambling were not enforced. I cooperated with Tom Speers, the marshall. He kept as much law and order as the townsfolk could tolerate.

And men, whether prosperous townsfolk or Western visitors, found their pleasures in the bustling city. After they had eaten and drunk and gambled at Marble Hall or one of the saloons on Market Square, they walked a few blocks to my cottages.

I remember one night in particular at the old houses. The cold was so fierce the river had frozen solid. I looked out of the front door's oval glass and felt the cold seeping in around the edges. It was frosted over except for a small kidney-shaped peephole in the center. I could see my breath this close to the door, although the rest of the house was warm and bright.

I glanced at Val Hayes. He sat in a straight-backed chair just outside the parlor. His large hands rested on his vast thighs. He seemed to be listening to the droning harmonium, half asleep in the dark hallway. This gargantuan man, kindly and gentle to those he knew, would come alert at the least sound out of order. He rested motionless, like a giant cat drowsing at a mousehole.

I must have been about 28 or 29 then, a large, well-fleshed woman, nearly six feet tall in my French-heel slippers, but Val Hayes towered over me. I had seen him pick up two combatants from the Turkish carpet and carry them both out the front door like sacks of potatoes.

I walked down the hall to the kitchen, nodded to Dora Hayes, Val's wife. Not enough business tonight to worry about running out of glasses, food or drink. Dora smiled, her plump face calm and competent. She smoothed her apron over her gingham dress and went about washing up from supper. I must remind Val to bring in more wood, I thought. The cold night sucked the warmth up the chimneys.

I went back and stood by the gingerbread of the doorway. I remember the deep neckline of the velvet dress I wore — my bosom rode high in its frame of tulle shirring. The short sleeves emphasized my arms. My corset shaped a waist still small. The crimson fabric of the plain underskirt hung straight to the toes of my shoes in front, but the overskirt was puffed and gathered over a bustle in back. I can remember the sway of the ball fringe. My blond hair was piled high on the back of my head and a single ringlet brushed my shoulder. I felt drop earrings of gold and garnet swing when I moved my head. I was beginning to grow nearsighted and kept a pair of prince-nez hidden in my pocket. I tended to frown a bit which make me look severe, so people said. I went into the parlor to make sure all was going as usual.

Mabel's slippered feet pumped the pedals on the reedy harmonium so that the lamps trembled on their sconces. She lifted her hands from the keys and the girls and the men in dark suits clapped. She slid off the bench, shivered, then pulled a fringed shawl up on her shoulders. Her violet-blue eyes were striking with her black hair and smooth olive skin. The fine cambric of her chemise gathered into a lace yoke. She joined Ada, Violet and Sally on the big settee. There were only two customers so far that night, both businessmen in sack coats of dark serge buttoned high on their chests, showing only a bit of their silk cravats. They had arrived about ten and seemed in no hurry to make their choices. The girls sat demurely on the big plush settee and chatted as if they, too, only wanted to sing and sip wine all evening.

No reason to hurry them along. Outside a piercing wind blew up off the river. The girls sat with their knees together, the plackets of their pantaloons still discreetly closed. Even open drawers could be modest.

Then I caught a movement in the corner of my eye of Violet brandishing a cigar, but then she handed it to one of the men. She had been lighting it for him. No hard liquor, no swearing, no roughhouse and the girls never smoked in the parlor. Violet had lit the cigar to tease me. She was high-spirited and her jokes livened the evening. She was thin and horsey and could sit on her flaxen hair when it was brushed out. But tonight it was puffed, teased, braided and swirled into a style she had copied from my *Harper's Bazaar*. It was an impressive structure to wear with muslin pantaloons with ribbons at the knees.

Sally, the youngest girl, pulled a satin sacque more tightly around her shoulders. In a plain dimity underwaist and drawers she looked even younger than her sixteen years. She seemed too quiet, so I motioned her to come and led her from the room.

"Are you well, Sally?" I asked.

"I'm all right, ma'am," Sally replied. She was so thin it seemed her neck could scarcely support the riot of auburn curls. The she coughed.

"Oh, Sally, you mustn't sit in the drafty parlor if you're coming sick." I laid my hand on her shoulder. This would be the last winter in this drafty little house. In three days, it would begin.

"I don't feel bad, honest," Sally said.

"If you take cold, you'll lose more than one night of customers. I'll have Dora make you some camomile tea. Go put on a warm nightgown and I'll bring the tea over."

The girls' rooms were in the frame house next door,

connected by the wooden hallway. Soon, there would be a better arrangement.

When I took the tea to Sally's room, the mauve sacque, bloused low in back, hung neatly behind the door. I put the tea on the bedside table and rested my hand on the girl's forhead. It was warm. I looked down her throat, saw redness and noted the fatigue in her eyes.

"Drink this while it's hot." When the girl finished, I pulled up the comforter. Her eyelids were already heavy.

"A good night's sleep is all you need."

I went to my room and consulted my book to see which remedy was best for sore throat. Some rest, wait and see. The patent medicines at the Golden Seven Drug Store were rarely as effective as they promised.

Before I reached the main house, I heard the wheels of a carriage stop outside. Val rose to answer the door as I took the teacup to the kitchen. "More business," I told Dora, now sitting in a rocker by the cast iron cookstove.

"Where's Annie?" a heavy male voice boomed. I tried to place the voice, but not until I saw the ruddy cheeks and drooping mustache above the buffalo robe did I realize who it was.

"Why Bill, how are you? I haven't seen you since last summer. Where've you been keeping yourself?"

Bill grabbed me around the waist and swung me off my feet.

"Working hard and thinking of you," he said and squeezed.

"Put me down, you big galoot!"

"I've been freezing my arse getting the freight to Santa Fe in the snow," he said.

"The railroad goes as far as Salina," I said. I enjoyed his bluster, but let him know he wasn't putting anything over on me.

"Who do you think humps the freight over the mountains from there?" countered Bill.

A shorter man with wiry red hair stood silently nearby.

Bill introduced him as Jack. The man bowed shyly and I took their coats and led them into the parlor where all conversation had stopped.

"Hey, Mabel, you still play that organ-thing?"

"Surely do, Bill." She rose and went to the harmonium.

"Play me 'Buffalo Gal' and get me some whiskey."

"Beer or wine?" I asked.

"Oh, wine, if that's the best you can do." Bill stood motionless for a moment after the song started, then began to sing, "Come out tonight, come out tonight." He tapped his boot in time to the music.

> Buffalo Gal, won't you come out tonight,
> Come out tonight,
> Come out tonight,
> Buffalo Gal, won't you come out tonight
> And dance by the light of the moon?

Bill grabbed Violet and began a heavy clog dance. She held on to his shoulders and dodged his boots with graceful hops as she sang and laughed to the song.

> Come out tonight,
> Come out tonight
> And dance by the light of the moon . . . .

Mabel sang the verses in a bird-high soprano and they all joined in on the chorus. One of the early customers pulled Ada, the fourth girl, to the floor. Her Indian-straight hair fell in a fan down her back. As she danced, the lace yoke of her chemise slipped from one plump shoulder and her breasts bobbed beneath the fine muslin.

"Play 'Camptown Races'," shouted Bill. He downed a glass of claret in one gulp and grabbed the breathless Violet again.

Camptown ladies sing this song
Doo Dah, Doo Dah, (Bill bellowed)
Camptown racetrack five mile long,
Oh! Doo Dah day!

And we all joined in.

Bill danced Violet down the hall to the kitchen door and back, then motioned me to join him.

I laughed and held up my arms. "Keep those clodhoppers off my slippers," I warned.

"I'll do better'n that," he replied. He fell backwards into a chair and began to unlace his boots. The other men took his cue and pulled off their elastic-sided shoes.

Mabel began a fast-tempo version of "Listen to the Mocking Bird" and followed with "O Susanna." We flew around the little parlor, singing and occasionally bumping into each other—Bill and me; his friend Jack with Ada, her black hair flying like a sail; and one of the early customers with Violet. We stomped and stepped until the lamps trembled on the tables. Another bottle of wine vanished.

In a pause in the music Sally appeared in the doorway, rubbing her eyes. In the red flannel nightdress she looked like a child disturbed by the parents' party.

"Who's this little lady?" boomed Bill as he turned from me.

"I didn't want to miss the fun," said Sally with a little girl's grin. Bill opened his arms wide and she hurried to him. He lifted her as he would a child and she snuggled into his broad chest with a sigh.

Mabel played a few bars of "Beautiful Dreamer" and we all laughed.

"Do you know 'Believe Me If All Those Endearing Young Charms'?" asked Jack. Mabel nodded and began the introduction. Jack listened closely, then began:

> Believe me if all those endearing young charms,
> Which I gaze on so fondly today,
> Were to fade by tomorrow and fleet in my arms
> Like fairy gifts fading away."

A pure, clear tenor voice poured from his scraggly throat. Everyone in the room paused as the romantic melody caught them.

> Thou wouldst still be adored
> As this moment thou art.
> Let thy loveliness fade as it will.
> And around the dear ruin
> Each wish of my heart
> Shall entwine itself verdantly still.

His voice rose, caressing each note, soaring and true. He raised goosebumps on my arms. By the time he finished the last verse I had pulled my handkerchief out of my pocket. Ada was openly sniffling. Mabel stood up from the bench and shook Jack's hand, too overcome for words. Even Bill blinked and blew his nose. I went to the harmonium and nudged Mabel toward the only customer still without a partner. It looked like it might be a good night after all. Bill and Jack sang a raucous duet of "Sweet Betsy from Pike," burlesquing its bathos. I loved men like Bill who brought a breath of the prairie, stirred up the girls and made us all laugh. Men who never asked the price because they had plenty of money. I played some soft songs and the men and women swayed in dreamy circles around the little parlor. The conversation fell to whispers and two by two the couples left the parlor.

Val cleared away the glasses and bottles, then took his place in the hall and listened, drowsing again, as I filled the silence with the comforting music.

Winter 1871

Just three days later I signed the papers for the new house. Some of the prosperous men I knew agreed to put up the money and I got ready to go to the bank. It was very important to look correct that day. I twisted in the pier glass to see if my dress was arranged properly. The black woolen overskirt must hang in precise gathers over the horsehair bustle. There was no way to disguise the bosom, so I let the stays out as much as I could to lessen the emphasis.

The bank officers would be there. And my lawyer. And Ermine Case, who was conveying the real estate. And the builder and his lawyer. Today I would commit myself to the construction of the house, a grand establishment and these two frame cottages would come down to make room. The title was clear and the lot already paid for. Only signing the papers was left.

I thought: My money is the same color as anybody else's.

I debated about powder and a bit of rouge, but no, I must look absolutely honest and upright. I reminded myself I was a business woman. I run this circus. I order, hire, fire, decide. I have made money. I did it myself. Now I'm taking on a bigger risk.

I leaned close to the glass to adjust my hat. My hair was piled high in back so that the hat tilted forward. Ribbons cascaded down the back.

I need more sleep, I thought as I noted the dark circles under my eyes. I was making myself scared. Silly woman, I thought. You are smart, lucky and hardworking. You have nothing to feel ashamed of. But my hands shook.

It was as though there were two Annies — one who wore décolleté velvet in the night; one who wore black alpaca and did business in the daytime. There had been other Annies, but they were dead. This Annie was the business woman, ready to face the respectable daytime people.

I tugged the front of the basque smartly, picked up my gloves and walked to the front door and stood where I could see Edwin Stewart's trap when he arrived.

We could easily walk the few blocks to the bank, but Ned had decreed that we must arrive in style.

My feet hurt in the button-top shoes. I wanted another cup of coffee. With brandy. Did I have a clean handkerchief? When would Ned arrive?

At last I saw his bays trot around the corner. I slipped into a heavy gabardine dolman and tucked a scarf around my throat. The overcast day blurred the hills across the river and I shivered in the damp wind.

It was the new year of 1871 and a good time to start a new project. A flock of pigeons whirled around the bluffs to the south, a grey flutter against the rocky cliffs. They whirled and dipped, rode the updrafts and dived again. I took them for a good omen and smiled. Stewart got his rig turned around and he reached down for me.

"Well, Annie, are you ready?"

"You're my lawyer. You tell me."

"I think everything is going to work out just fine."

"Very well, Ned. Let's get started," I said. "I'm going to

build the biggest, fanciest, best, most expensive sporting house between St. Louis and Sacramento."

"Your most obedient servant," he said with a satirical bow. He gee'd the horses and headed downhill to the bank.

Ice floes clotted the river. It had been the worst winter in memory, the river solid ice for seven weeks. It was starting to break up, but I wouldn't be surprised if it froze over again. One night three young men boasted they'd walked over the ice from Harlem, the little town on the north bank of the river.

The trap rattled and shook as it rolled over the vitreous paving bricks. We turned from Third and went down Delaware to the bank at Fifth.

Wood smoke mingled with the morning fog. As we passed the intersection I caught glimpses of Market Square, alive with activity in the January morning. Several prairie schooners were anchored in the open area. The number of horses tied up at the police station made me wonder what was going on.

Tom Speers, the marshall, and I had reached an understanding. There was talk of reorganizing the police force and I hoped I wouldn't have to start over again and break in a new man. Speers had flatly said he wouldn't bother me as long as my house was not "unruly." I paid a fine of $30 a month for operating a disorderly house and $20 a month for the sale of wine and beer. Plus court costs. Virtually an operating license. All very regular. No protection and no kickbacks.

"I serve no hard liquor, Mr. Speers," I had said. "Only wine and beer. My girls behave genteely. This inspires good manners. My prices keep the riffraff out."

"Genteel manners may not be enough," Speers countered. "You keep order among your employees and, er, customers, madam, and you will not hear from me. Except, of course, a purely symbolic closing, with much public outcry, a month before an election." He brushed the edges of his drooping mustache and watched me to see if I understood.

"Val Hayes, my houseman, is quite strong," I answered. "He's six feet, seven inches, a regular Goliath. His wife, Dora, is my housekeeper. We can keep an orderly house."

Speers nodded. He stood just inside the door of the little house. He had not removed his hat. His cavalier attitude would continue as long as everything stayed under control.

"You may count on me, Mr. Speers," I had said. "You are always welcome, as a private citizen, of course." I tried not to smile.

Speers tipped his hat and left.

The city streets buzzed with mercantile activity. Wagons rattled over the brick and macadam. Messenger boys dashed in and out of buildings, their cheeks ruddy and eyes bright. A few women in furs lifted their skirts to enter Burr & Falconer's dry goods store. A little too heavy to work for me, I thought. I always sized up respectable women, my private game. Then I only had the four girls and Mabel planned to leave soon. I preferred girls fresh from the country, healthy, not too heavy, and biddable. I never actively recruited girls, but some unknown fate doled me sufficient to stay in business.

Ned tied up in front of the First National Bank and ran around to help me out. I stood on the wooden sidewalk while he bribed a boy to watch the rig and I shivered again in the dismal wind that blew up the street and cut through my gabardine. Ned offered his arm and we walked up the iron steps into the bank lobby. I wished then that Ned were older, didn't grin so much, was weightier in demeanor. Dear Ned. I walked straight into the president's office, looking neither to right nor left, shoulders straight, head high, then paused just inside the door. Mort Dively, the president of the bank, sat at his rolltop desk. Beside him were Holden, the cashier, and Allen, the vice president, and a cadre of blank-faced clerks. B. F. Nicholas, the builder, sat in another corner at a table covered with plans. His attorney, whom I didn't know, sat beside him and next to him stood Ermine Case.

The men rose; I bowed to each. I took a seat beside Ned. I wished I had something to hold on to—a pen, a piece of paper, someone's hand. My knees shook and I was dry-mouthed. To keep my hands from shaking, I clasped a handkerchief.

This is just a business affair, I reminded myself. They don't care as long as they can see the color of your money. I remembered the stir when I first went to Dively with the plans. He was dumbfounded that the owner of a fancy house had the backing to do what I proposed. All I needed was someone to arrange the contracts, handle the payments and keep books, all legal.

"Gentlemen, shall we begin?" My voice came out too loud. I cleared my throat and clasped my hands more firmly. "I think we should start with Mr. Nicholas's plans. I wish to go over them one more time, then Mr. Stewart and I would like to change the wording on the clause regarding the kitchen fixtures."

Nicholas, a beefy man with a broad face, placed a Venice glass paperweight on one corner of a huge sheet of plans, held the other down with a callused hand. I bent over the table and counted, for perhaps the fifteenth time, the number and location of the rooms. Sixteen bedrooms on the second floor and four bathrooms; my suite of wine parlor and bedroom on the first floor; dining room, three parlors, music room and ballroom, also on the first floor; and kitchen and storage in the cellar.

"Four bathrooms are mighty extravagant, Miss Annie," suggested the builder.

"And two more on the first floor," I replied. "A necessary extravagance."

"A fireplace in every room?"

"And why not?"

"You could leave the servants' rooms without."

"No."

"Very well. Gaslights in every room. We install the pipes and you install the fixtures."

"Did you put more outlets in the hall upstairs? It will be very dark without."

"Yes, ma'am."

"Has the contract been amended to specify top grade walnut in the wainscoting? I want no skimping."

"Yes, ma'am. And short lengths of white oak for the floors."

"The mirrors for the ballroom?"

"Ordered to size."

"Have you decided how to make the concrete pillars for the entry?"

"We're building the forms now. I'm not sure how they're going to look. I never saw pillars made to look like giant bamboo."

"They'll blend in with the pagoda roof on the porch."

"Cast ironwork is in the contract, but the railings won't be made until the rest is in place."

"Let me look at the kitchen plans one more time while Mr. Stewart reads the contract."

"We've made all the changes you requested," protested Nicholas.

"Then reading will verify that." I gave him a hard look but my damp hands gripped the handkerchief more tightly. "Mr. Stewart, please."

I pulled the pince-nez out of my pocket so I could see details. Ned began to read from the contract and I checked to make sure every written order had its counterpart on the drawings. When Stewart finished reading, I initialed the plans.

Then Dively and his officers and the three black-coated acolytes arranged the contracts across the desk. Each party in turn signed the papers. Stewart had gone over each one carefully and had assured me that all was correct. This was a $100,000 commitment, not lightly undertaken. Years of work to get this far; more years to make it succeed.

"An extravagant establishment," said Dively as I put on my gloves. I shook each man's hand in turn. I felt like congratulations, whether they did or not. The acolytes' eyes widened in amazement.

"My customers are used to the very best. The extravagance is for their convenience. You wouldn't want to be inconvenienced, would you, Mr. Dively?" He colored and looked away and I bit my lips to keep from smiling.

The damp handkerchief, edges tatted and faintly cologned, stiffened in the chill wind.

"Find me a hack and you won't have to make the trip back, Ned," I said.

"Just as soon do that as sit in my office reading."

"Not too many customers?"

"Please, we call them clients."

"Of course."

"We young attorneys have more time to spend with our clients. When I'm old and important, you won't be able to spend five minutes with me."

"It's a bit early for lunch, but Dora should have something working by now. Won't you join us and warm up?"

"Thank you kindly, Annie."

"Aren't you afraid that consorting with a scarlet woman will ruin your reputation?" I mocked.

"The women in town don't know who you are and the men are afraid to admit they do."

"Likely."

"Besides, I shall never abandon my efforts. As you are my client, I want you to make me your client."

I bristled, but did not speak. Ned assumed I turned tricks, but I did not. He was a comely fellow, tall and blue-eyed, with a sandy shock of hair which fell over his forehead. He always joshed me and never took anything seriously if he could help it, back then.

He was a smart contrast to Ermine Case, who handled the real estate part of the transaction. Where Ned was bluff, ruddy and brash, Ermine was thin, sickly and restrained. My contact with Case was business only; I'm not sure he even knew my profession. But take him as a sample of the kind of prosperous men I knew in the city. I think Ermine probably had TB, even then, and didn't know it. He wasn't as prominent a citizen as his brother, Theodore Case, who came to Kansas City before he war and was chief quartermaster of the District of the Border. Theodore was on the board of everything and had his finger in every pie. Ermine specialized in real estate. He held my property from January of 1871 until February 17, 1873, when the note was finally paid.

Ermine read law in Ohio before he came to Missouri after the war. He secured the funds for the building to house the Young Men's Christian Association and was an active promoter of the Law and Order League. He was trustee and treasurer of the Second Presbyterian Church and president of the YMCA when he died at 47. Like most of the prosperous people of that time, he lived on Quality Hill, the best neighborhood, in a large brick residence with a carriage house. He was ordinary-looking with a thin face and narrow shoulders, thin light hair and a drooping mustache. I always think of him as faded compared to his brother.

Upstanding as he was, he was typical of the prosperous men who advised me, backed me and patronized my resort. I have never been indiscreet. I always referred to them as my "prosperous men," as some still have family living in Kansas City today.

My house was as well ordered as theirs. The food was probably better; the wine certainly was. And they could put their feet up and smoke cigars, spit, scratch or swear. They could play cards all night or take a girl upstairs.

There were men lustier than Ermine then. It didn't take long to become a prosperous pillar of that raw city. These

were men who had, a few years before, ridden with Jo
Selby's cavalry or Thomas Moonlight's or fought with Ster-
ling Price or Samuel Curtis. The war really started on the
Missouri-Kansas border in 1856 and sometimes I think it's
still going on. I have a friend who thinks Lawrence should
be burned annually, and the James brothers canonized.

I knew the Jameses, of course. The city was small
enough then that everyone knew almost everyone. I
bought china and glassware from their uncle's company
and I knew Zee's father, who ran a hotel in Harlem, north
of the river. Jesse came to my house several times, in the
company of that drunken newspaper hack, John Newman
Edwards. They were more interested in talk than the girls,
since a resort is a good place to pass along information.

Many of my clients still carried sidearms, although that
was fading as the city became a little tamer. But the men
weren't tame. They turned their energies to raising money
back East for real estate and mining, risked thousands in
businesses like the stockyards, which grew weekly, it
seemed, in the West Bottoms. They traded like demons on
the livestock market, born gamblers. Others spent years on
bleak cavalry outposts fighting Indians only to come back
and find themselves bound by the conventions of propriety and gentility imposed by the well-bred women of their
class. Suddenly, a man whose early years had been active
was choking in his silk cravat and broadcloth suit. Choking
on propriety.

Then they came to my sporting house for women bound
neither by steel stays or ordinary conventions. It was a
prosperous men's club as much as a bordello, with a careful
madam, clean girls and luxurious surroundings.

I provided a service to my customers. I demanded
respect and gave it. I liked many of the men who patronized my establishment and became friends with some of
them. If I had a jaundiced view of johns in general, I kept
it to myself.

But Ned didn't know that. There was scarcely enough

time to greet the customers, see to the refreshments, keep an eye on the girls and make sure there was enough clean linen. I rose before anyone but Dora and was up until the last customer left. There was no time to turn tricks, but Ned assumed I did.

"If I ever decide to take a lover, Ned," I said, "you'll be the first." I kept my voice light. "I've been a mistress and a madam, but never a whore." Forget the details, it had a nice rhythm to it.

Ned started to say something to dispute me, then realized that the words, similar in meaning, were different.

"All right, Annie," he responded after a bit. "As long as I'm the first in line."

I reached over and patted his arm. "Dear Ned. A friend like you is a blessing."

When we arrived back at the house I checked with Dora and re-issued my invitation for lunch. I went to my room to take off hat and gloves. When we were seated in the little dining room off the front parlor, Ned, with a mischievous grin said, "You've been a mistress and a madam, you say."

I nodded.

"When were you a mistress?"

"None of your business, Mr. Knowitall. Mind your manners or you'll be eating cold sandwiches at your desk instead of Dora's bean soup with ham and good cornbread."

The girls straggled in *en negligée* and helped themselves.

"Did you know Mollie Smart had a party last week?" asked Ned. Cornbread crumbs bobbed on his mustache. Mollie was another madam over on Fourth Street.

"Yes," I said. "I took several girls and went over to see how it was going. There were only nine men."

"Probably not enough people heard about it."

Dora poured coffee, then cut wedges of dried apple pie for everyone.

"I bought a bottle of wine, we drank it and came home," I said. "I bet I could give a better party."

"That's a good idea," Ned answered. The girls sitting close enough to hear nodded in agreement.

"I get more than nine customers most nights, anyway."

"Yes, but if you got lots of men, I mean everybody, to come to your party, why that'd make sure people didn't forget you while your new house is abuilding."

"I'll have invitations printed," I said, getting into the spirit.

"But you can't mail them to their homes," Ned warned.

"Everybody's listed in Hoye's commercial directory. I'll mail the invitations to their businesses and mark them Personal."

"When do they tear these houses down?"

"Next week."

"Well, get those invitations out!"

The night of the party 108 men showed up. That's how many I collected from. I had to call police headquarters to send over two men in uniform to keep order. We ran through my supply of wine and exhausted the kegs I had on hand. Maude Dunham came over and asked if she could help. I said yes and she brought over her girls and two more kegs of beer. My girls—Violet, Mabel, Ada and Sally—turned tricks as fast as they could get up and down the stairs. People were dancing in the street to a music box Maude set up on a packing case outside the houses. It was as though the party was a snowball which had started down from the top of a big hill and rolled faster and got bigger as the night went on. I was so busy, I didn't pay any attention to how much I was drinking and soon I was skimming along, not caring what happened.

Ned Stewart kept swinging me around the parlor in a dance that only he knew the steps to. I laughed and danced and for once stopped worrying about what was going on. Thurmond Chester, called Bubba, slipped on some spilled wine and went through the parlor window. That set everyone wild and the johns and the girls threw shoes, glasses, whatever they could find and broke out the windows on the ground floor. Each tinkle of breaking glass was followed by a roar of approval. It was winter and the street dancers dodged piles of grey and re-frozen snow, but the fresh air was welcome in the crowded rooms. There was scarcely enough room to move.

All my backers and all my prosperous men were there, it seemed, and either nodded or came to speak to me. Ned hovered nearby, pitched in when the policemen needed help, and otherwise acted as my escort for the evening. I pulled tulle frills off my skirt as they came loose and tossed them away. I would have danced barefoot but for the broken glass. I only wished that Bill and his friend could be there, or Ambrose Leary or Frank Greathouse, but they were all out on the winter prairie somewhere.

When the sun rose, the party broke up. First the men began trickling away in twos and threes to catch the first streetcars from the trolley barn around he corner, then the girls, a pretty bedraggled bunch they were by then, went to their still-warm beds to curl up under as many comforters and quilts as they could find, since the house was cold. Maude and her girls thanked me and went off to their own house.

I never remembered inviting him, but I woke up about ten that morning with Ned in my bed. And right glad I was to have him. The broken windows made the house as cold as the February outdoors and as much champagne as I had had, I might have frozen to death in my sleep.

I slipped out of bed and counted the money that I had stuck in a drawer. I went over my bills and figured the costs of the party and after I paid all the bills, I would still have $645 left. I put the cash in a band box and went back to bed.

"Wake up, sleepy head," I said to Ned and shook him a little.

He had been awake a while and was playing possum. He grabbed me and kissed me and hopped out of bed to use the chamber pot, then hopped back in. It was so cold we could see our breath.

"Why is it so cold in here?" he asked.

"We broke out the windows last night. Don't you remember?"

"Can't say I do. What else?"

"Dancing in the street? Maude's girls. Policemen?"

"Oh, yes."

"Don't you need to get to work?"

"I think I'll take the day off."

"Never get rich that way."

"I've got something I always wanted right here."

"How'd you talk me into letting you into my bed?" I asked.

"Didn't talk. Just did it."

"What did I do?"

"Went to sleep as soon as you hit the sheets."

"Here I was feeling bad because there'd been a big time and I didn't remember it."

"You could make it a big time, right now," Ned suggested.

"So I could."

I reached over and ran my hands through his unruly sandy hair, then stroked down his strong neck and shoulders. I smoothed his mustache and started unbuttoning his undershirt. We didn't want to get out from under the covers, so we thrashed around under the tepee of blankets. I knew his face and his hands already, and now I set out to learn the rest of him. Our heads were out of the blankets and the rest of us was inside. We were two blind people, each searching the other for what we wanted. It was as though we must touch and rub and nuzzle every inch of the other's body before we would be satisfied. Ned came in the sheets when his head was between my legs. I told him to share it with his friends, so after we had explored every possible stretch of skin, every crease, every patch of hair, he entered and I forgot myself, forgot every whore's trick, forgot every bit of finesse I ever knew and bucked like an unbroken filly.

He came again as I came and when he withdrew, noticed I still thrummed to his rhythm. He cupped me and I orgasmed again, then he began to see what would set me off. The climaxes built and built and I thought I would go on forever, until the flesh grew tender and the pain was greater than the pleasure.

We stayed in the warm, sticky tepee until we got so cold we had to get more clothes on or freeze. Dora and Val heated bath water for us and whipped up some kind of breakfast for Ned and me and the girls.

"You look like a cat in the cream," he said as we spooned down steaming outmeal. "What're you thinking?"

"Wondering if you'll talk to your friends."

"Do you care?"

"That's the least of my cares."

"I won't, though, if you don't want it."

"That's considerate of you, Ned."

I hadn't realized how long I'd been lonely until I woke up with Ned. I hoped he'd keep coming back. I was getting older and I didn't want to be alone. He wasn't Richmond, but I'd never have Richmond. Ned was hearty good fun.

Dora and Val Hayes found a temporary place with a family north of the city and I stayed at the St. Nicholas Hotel until the new house was habitable. But first, I went to New York and Chicago to choose the furnishings for the new house. I wanted nothing but the best. Quadruple plate silver serving pieces, thick Persian carpets. I engaged craftsmen to do the ornamental plastering around the ceilings and the pressed tin designs on the arches over the entrance to the ballroom. I chose material for the draperies and spreads, ordered enough bone china and bed linen for a first class hotel. Ormulu clocks. Gilt sconces. And a huge crystal chandelier for the ballroom.

When I was in Chicago, I visited an artist to select oil paintings. I wanted something that would fit in with my business. The nude figure is not necessarily pornographic but the one with the bear came close. The artist kept regular business hours and greeted me in a sober black suit and silk waistcoat. I had expected some bohemian smock and flowing tie, but he was just like any other merchant selling his wares. I liked that. I realized when I traveled how insular my existence was, compared to the larger world.

"Madam," he said, "I have pulled out several paintings which you might like to see." He indicated there larger-than-life nudes on easels and propped against the walls. I stopped at one which showed a voluptuous blond with her left arm thrown over her head.

"Good Lord!" he said.

"What is it?"

He danced around and looked at me, then pushed me over to the painting so he could see both it and me side by side.

"That looks, um, somewhat like you, madam."

I stared at it again. It did, a little. Blond hair, blue eyes, full figure.

"I couldn't buy that painting. People would think I posed for it."

"Very interesting, though, wouldn't you agree?"

I hadn't told him what I did for a living, but he might have guessed by my choice of paintings.

"Still, it is an amazing coincidence."

I wandered on around the room. The grey Chicago sun shown through the high windows and skylight, patching the bare room with daylight. In one corner, a canvas covered with a cloth rested on a paint-stained easel. A table with pots and brushes gave off a steady breath of turpentine. The painter followed me around, available for questions, his hands clasped behind his back.

I ordered two paintings and then wandered back to the blond nude. People might think I posed for it. Well, let them think that. It might boost my reputation and certainly couldn't hurt it.

"Mr. Gross," I said.

"Yes, madam?"

"Do you ever touch up a painting once you've finished?"

"Well, sometimes. It depends. What did you have in mind?"

"This painting would look even more like me if her nose were a bit longer. What do you think?" I backed over so he could see both of us again.

"Yes, and perhaps the chin a bit stronger. You wish me to make it *more* like you?"

"If it wouldn't offend you to change your work."

"On the contrary, madam, I am fascinated. It is as though I did the painting and it was waiting for you to find it. Let me make a few sketches."

He sat me down in the light near his work table and scratched on a pad with a soft pencil. After a while we decided on prices and delivery and I sashayed back out onto the street. I remember that visit as windy, of course, but full of good memories. That painting looked the way I'd like to look.

At another gallery I bought steel engravings: "The Turning of the Drove"—of longhorn cattle and a herd dog in a winter pasture. "The Return"—of a soldier and his girl. And "The Refusal"—a sad young woman holding a letter. They were sentimental, but people liked them. I always had Western scenes for the military men and cattlemen.

One of my special prosperous friends accompanied me to New York and we saw the shows and ate at the fancy places. I looked and remembered so that my resort would be as good as anything in the East.

I got back to town and took a room at the St. Nicholas. When I could take time from supervising the workmen, I ordered lunch sent up and Ned joined me for a warm afternoon.

Besides all the things I was having installed and moved in, there was a most important item: a buzzer under the stairs that ran straight to the police station so I could summon help if things got out of hand.

I spent so much money on the furnishings and decorations that I had to go to my backers for more money to pay the workmen after construction began. But I knew quality would pay in the long run.

The house was an L, the entry square in the middle of the Third Street side. From there, once you entered, you could go right to the west parlor or straight ahead up the stairs or left to the long side of the L. On the east side were the main parlor, the ballroom and the dining room. My quarters were down the hall on the east side, toward the back of the house. I had a huge bedroom, an alcove where I kept my desk and files and a small room I called the wine parlor. It was only 8' x 8', but it was a room where I could receive private visitors or do business away from the flurry of the house. The kitchen was in the basement and the housekeeper and houseman had their apartment down there. The girls' rooms and a few storage rooms were on the second floor.

While they raised the house I took the Union Pacific as far as Denver, then went on to Santa Fe. I liked to visit other madams and we were on good terms. We traded information and sometimes girls went back and forth. When I saw how harsh the frontier life was, away from the cities, I decided that my place would be warm and comfortable, a place of softness and pleasure. The colors were mostly vermillion and gilt with royal blue. It was rich and bright, clean and lively.

I opened for business that summer, about six months after the old houses were torn down. Now I worried about making it pay. I owed thousands to my backers. They invested in me the same as they would in any new business, expecting me to show a profit. I was as good a businessman as they and they treated me respectfully because of it. It was a long two years before I was in the black, but Ermine Case finally filed the deed in the Jackson County courthouse on February 17, 1873, two years and a little more after we first signed the papers.

But that summer of '71 the house wasn't finished. People kept after me to re-open. While workmen traipsed through the dust, girls came to ask to work for me. I had as many as sixteen girls at capacity, but I think I started with fewer than ten. My girls had the reputation for being the best in town — not the most beautiful, but the most cultivated. I taught them manners and cleanliness, sometimes feeling as though I were still the school teacher. I took them to good dressmakers for the latest styles. We frequently had to alter them somewhat so the girls could get them on and off easily. There was no straggling about in the parlor *en negligée* anymore. I didn't always have much to start with, but I encouraged them to save their money and stay off the booze and many went from my house to become good citizens. So many were down and out when they arrived that it made me especially proud when one left with a good nest egg, holding her head up.

About this time there arrived a young girl wearing cowhide boots, home-knitted stockings and a calico slip. She was dusty and rumpled, probably from the train, but the poor shapeless slip had been washed and starched until it cracked. In her hand was a cardboard suitcase.

It was my policy to question every girl who appeared at my place to learn all that I could about them. I had decided early never to admit one from Kansas City, since it would be a source of much annoyance to me and embarrassment to her relatives.

This girl stood before me in the entryway. The floor tiles

which spelled out my last name were shiny and the grout was still white.

All the girls who came to me were either determined or desperate. I had to judge whether they would also fit in and do the work or not. Sometimes I could dissuade the not-so-desperate and give them train fare home. I had just seen to the wrought iron bars on the windows on the street side of the building. Some said it was to keep the girls from committing suicide. I never kept girls against their will; they were not good workers and I was not interested in running a prison. I took my losses and let them go. The bars were to keep cheaters from skipping out without paying for extras.

This girl in the calico slip seemed calm and determined.

"What's your name, child?"

"Belle Waterman."

"Where are you from?"

"A farm, by Knob Noster." She looked like a farm girl whose natural delicacy hadn't been hardened by too many years of heavy work and harsh sun. Her face was naturally beautiful, with delicate features and coloring like sunlight through rose petals. Her voice had the country sound of soft endings.

"What do you want?"

Just then a dray stopped outside the front door and the superintendent came up the steps.

"We're bringing this big mirra in today, ma'am. The carpenter is here to build the frame. Lordy, lordy, it's the biggest mirra I ever hauled."

I left Belle to watch the unloading of the French beveled glass. It had cost a lot in the first place, then it cost a lot more to ship it.

The men eased it off the wagon bed and carried it into the room that would be the ballroom. When they put it down and left, I went back to the girl.

"You want to enter this place. Do you know that it is a whore house?"

She nodded. "I know what this place is and I have heard that you are a fair woman to work for."

"Why have you come?" I asked.

"My Pa turned me out, said it was time I made my own way. I decided this is the way I'll go."

She seemed too naive to know what she was doing. Yet, I remember making that same decision not many years before. There was something about her fair hair and soft skin, something that reminded me of myself. There were the same blue eyes, the same determination.

For an instant I could stand in her boots, making the step from everyday to The Life. I had been in The Life seven years. I had long ago jettisoned the genteel morality of the everyday world. I had seen people destroyed in the bordellos and I had seen more goodness than any moralizer could have imagined. I knew the conventions of the day for what they were—narrow, petty, paralyzing. I knew of women so moral they had turned their own daughters out like dogs, for a single error. Denied their own flesh and blood for fear of what the neighbors might say. I knew a man who begrudged his workers a ten-cent device that would make their jobs safer, then spent without thought at Madame Chevalier's establishment. I knew men whose wives thought sex was dirty and refused them. I knew people who sat through Sunday sermons after a Saturday night debauch.

I knew that what I did was against the law, against the commandments, against opinion. But I never thought the less of myself. I did something that needed doing and if a marriage failed, why blame it on the bordellos? If all the houses closed that day there would be no less coupling the next. I provided a service men were willing to pay for and I was doing it better than anyone else in town.

But it was as though all that blew away for a moment, like rose petals in a storm, and I could see the girl looking at The Life with new eyes, measuring it and deciding. I tried to make it easy for her to turn away because she seemed too innocent to know what she was doing. Rotten roses smell worse than offal because you remember their sweetness.

"This is a hard life," I warned. "You will have to make yourself agreeable whether you will or not, put up with rough men who have no thought for you except as they use you."

She only nodded.

Then the doorbell rang again and there was another wagonload of furnishings. The fixtures for the gaslamps arrived from the brassworks, along with spittoons for every room, railings, cleats for the carpet on the stairs and some other pieces I didn't recognize. I excused myself to check the invoice and tell the men where to put the brass items.

When I returned to the entry, the girl still stood quietly. She possessed a calm that few girls could show when they stood before me the first time. And she was patient, I had to give her credit for that.

"This is a hard life," I said again.

She nodded.

"There's always the danger of disease, although we're as careful as we can be. If you take the clap, you're ruined for the future, for children." I spoke firmly to her. I wanted to test her, to see if I thought she could take The Life. If she began wavering, I would know she was not cut out for it. But she only nodded.

"Drink is always a problem."

"I know about drinking," she said grimly.

"To be gay and drink with the customers makes it easy to learn the habit. There is cocaine, laudanum, morphine. You'll age ten times faster in this house if you're careless than doing the roughest housework somewhere else."

Still she nodded. She stood motionless in her shapeless clothes, wearing the ugliest overcoat I had ever seen. It looked to be a man's topcoat, but so old and worn it had no style left.

I really laid it on. I never tried to trick a girl into coming into my place, but rather tried to get rid of them. Some people think I had to force girls to come into The Life. Instead, I tried to make sure they were determined, then I respected their choice. I didn't always understand the reasons, but I had known so many girls that I felt I had seen it all, even though I wasn't yet thirty. Now I got down to the part which usually turned them away, if they were to be turned.

"You will be beaten and knocked about every night by the rough men who come here. I'll get in my own licks if you don't behave." This was a lie. I never permitted brawls. "Do you still want to stay?"

I can always remember the strong things, the pleasures and the losses, but I almost never remember exactly when I first had an idea. That day I can recall looking at Belle and thinking of myself and all the girls who stood for the first time before the madam.

I'm sure I had run through the ideas before, but this is the time I remembered each separate part.

Belle and I stood face to face. I remember her eyes didn't dart around or seek the shadows. She looked straight at me and that calm only wavered once, when I mentioned disease. I expected her to run away, but I didn't expect her to stand there with only a flicker of emotion.

Then I saw myself and The Life with her eyes and realized that to her, I was an old harridan, coarse and evil, the agent of wickedness. For a moment I felt the repugnance she felt, although she would never have deliberately revealed it to me. Proper virtuous women were allowed to feel that disgust because they were so well used to cultivating their virtue. It wasn't all spelled out in the etiquette books, especially in Kansas City where the forms weren't so rigid. Still, a lady knew who she was and what she was supposed to do. And whom she could despise.

She could cut a woman of her own station caught in sexual indiscretion. The proper woman wouldn't talk to the sinner or even acknowledge her presence by so much as a glance on the street. She would not invite the sinner to her home and could refuse to remain in her presence in public.

"Wayward" women were punished, but their partners were neither considered wayward nor punished. A proper woman could remove from her life a sinner of a class lower than hers. She could fire the housemaid, even if her husband or son had gotten the girl pregnant. She could refuse to keep a cook who didn't behave as she thought fit. She could cocoon herself in her own righteousness and keep the real world out, a world where women fall in love unwisely and girls give themselves foolishly.

To a virtuous woman I might be incomprehensible. A truly cocooned woman mightn't know bordellos existed or what they were for or that someone needed to manage them. And if she did, she would see them as a source of disease, not realizing that we were cleaner and more careful than she was because we weren't so ignorant. She might see the whole institution as a Social Vice, unavoidable but regrettable, and try to ignore the houses. A slightly more sophisticated virtuous woman might look on the houses and their inmates as a necessary evil. If she didn't like sex, she might privately be relieved that we absorbed her husband's unwanted attentions. If she were hot-blooded, she might hate us for taking his attention.

I don't think I would have minded it, the sneering of the virtuous women, if I hadn't seen the outcome of their virtue. Their means brought unjustified ends. Girls like Belle had nowhere to go. Women were hounded out of town, couldn't work, even as servants. Girls who had made a mistake, probably out of ignorance, were treated like the very spawn of the devil. Helping that girl instead of pushing her out, alone, in the world to have a baby that was somebody's grandchild—that would have been true virtue.

What did the virtuous woman offer those who wanted to change from streetwalking or even working in a house? Twelve hours a day of cleaning up after a family as a maid, emptying slops, scrubbing, washing, maybe doing the cooking and watching the children, all for a wage that didn't cover necessities. The virtuous women did not, however, hire their servants from the city workhouse. The women trying to reform weren't treated badly; they were ignored and left to starve or return to The Life.

I didn't think all these ideas in that instant when I talked to Belle, but I had thought them one at a time and that day they all seemed to hit me at once. I saw myself through somebody else's eyes and it was painful to own that I was hated and despised by some. It was true—I pandered. I was a pimp, for all my grand house and fancy furniture. I served the lowest urges of human nature. I oversaw prodigies of sinfulness and provided for it if I did not participate myself. I was sister to the whore of Babylon. I was the lowest of the low, but worse, I refused to stay low. I flaunted myself, appeared even to enjoy what I did, and sorry to say, showed fewer ill effects of living The Life than they did living in their cocoons. Some marriages were little more than a form of legalized prostitution.

I was a whore and a mistress and a pander and a madam. But I was no hypocrite.

I believed then and I still believe that I, notorious and wicked woman, did more good in my life than the virtuous women did in theirs. I had more chances, perhaps. I did my share of bad things, but hardly ever with the intention of doing someone a bad turn. I couldn't have lived if I hadn't thought I was a worthwhile person, at least by my own lights.

I looked at Belle and realized what I was and wanted something different for her.

"Do you still want to stay?"

"I'd be obliged," she said.

I shrugged and led her to a dingy little room that was barely inhabitable where I kept broken furniture and a spare bed. It had only a small, high window and it was crowded with boxes and trunks. No one could live in it. She said not a word, but put her suitcase on the bare floor and said, "I need some supper. It's last night since I ate. Then I'm ready to start."

I told her the dinner bell would sound and showed her the bathroom and the linen closet and left her because the doorbell rang again and there were curve-leg tables to distribute through the rooms. Any day the heavy leather chairs and couches would arrive. The next delivery that day was the circular settee. It was so big, it had to be dismantled in the wagon bed and brought it in pieces. Then the drayman returned to the furniture company to fetch a carpenter and upholsterer to reassemble it. I wanted no damage to the fine cut velvet. It took the rest of the afternoon.

Belle appeared in a heavy old nightgown that evening. Yards of faded flannelette covered her from chin to instep. I made the other girls hush their giggles and told her to stay in her room until I could find her something. I had patience with her because she had such a pretty face I knew she'd be popular. I told the housekeeper to find her a wrapper while I checked the kitchen and the parlors that night. Dora must have forgotten and I was distracted by early-arriving customers and the hundred invisible things I thought I had to keep track of in the unfinished house, so she didn't work that night.

The next night I told her just to sit in the parlor and get used to the way things went. I never pushed the girls at first. The inexperienced ones were scared and it gave the more practiced ones a breathing space. I wanted them to learn not to rush the customers, but learn to make themselves agreeable and entertaining. My house was as elegant as I could make it. The customers paid as they entered. The girl and I split the $5 fee 50–50. Food was gratis, wine and beer extra. They were on the honor system to report all their tricks since I refused the cheap brass tokens low class houses used. I could pretty well keep track of what was going on and the housekeeper recorded the clean linen each girl used.

A few days after she arrived Belle delivered a baby boy, all alone in that dreary room.

I don't often make a mistake like that. Maybe it was the bulky coat and the shapeless slip. Maybe it was her pretty face or the ideas all coming at once. Maybe it was the distraction of the deliverymen and movers. I was mad at her and mad at myself that I hadn't caught on when she first walked in the door.

The housekeeper called me up and I saw the scrawny little thing and his mother, sweaty and tired now.

"Child, why didn't you tell me?"

"I was afeared you wouldn't take me and I didn't have nowhere else to go. I'm right sorry, Miss Annie, but I didn't know what to do. I only heard about your place and I don't know a soul in this whole city." She began to cry and the tears rolled down her cheeks, but she kept looking at me.

"Once I've taken you on, you can stay." She started to thank me, but I said, "It's not charity. You'll be a good worker and we'll both come out ahead when you recover."

Tears still rolled down her face, but now she smiled.

"Tell me what really happened," I said.

She looked away, toward the high, dusty window, then back at me.

"Farm girls know how . . . animals mate. That's no big secret. My Pa's a hard man and my Ma's afeared of him. He beats her when he's been at the jug. I'd gone with some of the boys and it didn't seem like a big thing. Then one night, I was in my straw tick half asleep and my Pa came at me. He was drunk, but that don't change nothing. He stuffed my blanket in my mouth and did what he wanted to do. He said he'd kill me if I breathed a word."

Belle had stopped crying and her pretty face had gone hard. I didn't want to hear the story, but once started she needed to finish. I took her brush and smoothed back her fair hair as she lay on the pillow, where she couldn't see my face or my tears.

"I told Ma, but she didn't believe me. She whipped me for saying such things about my Pa. Then I missed my monthlies and pretty soon they noticed. My Pa drove me off the farm, told me I was trash. He was afeared for what would happen when the baby came, if it looked like him or if I could get somebody to believe me. He gave me a few dollars and told me never to come back. I heard some men from the town talking about this place when I wasn't supposed to hear, so this was the only place I knew to come. I thought I was ruined already and it wouldn't ruin me any more to work here."

There was nothing I could say. I had heard the story in a dozen variations and still did not have one thing to say. All I could do was try to comfort her. I called for clean sheets and some clear soup and helped Dora bathe her and the baby.

"You get well and then we'll see," I said. "You aren't ruined unless you think you are. You are a brave and strong girl and now you have that little one." I put my hand on the baby's tiny head, almost the size of Belle's milk-swollen breasts and I knew I could never turn her out.

"I'll pay you back, Miss Annie," she promised. "You'll never be sorry."

"I know, child."

I moved her to a better room, with more light and heat. It was late in the spring and the nights were still chilly. I checked on her every day and little by little I learned the hardness of her life. Her family had a cabin in the hills near Knob Noster. The farm barely supported the family, which included older and younger children as well as Belle and the parents. What little extra there was, the father drank up. She was used to sleeping in the unheated loft of the cabin; no wonder she didn't complain about the bad room I sent her to. She had only the one dress, some tattered underwear and that winter coat. I bought her what she needed and kept the ledger sheet, never expecting to get it back.

In the meantime, the house was getting finished. The day the china came the infant cried without cease. It put the deliverymen on edge and they dropped a crate of chamber pots. The noise surprised the child into a moment's silence, then he began again. Belle was exhausted. At first the other girls fussed over the baby and took it to give her some rest. He wasn't sickly, exactly, but colicky. Soon they began to complain and Belle had to take him down to the kitchen where he couldn't be heard.

I sorted through the broken crockery, salvaged about half the pots, and haggled with the deliveryman over recompense. His men carried the dinnerware to the dining room and the basins and pitchers and jars to the second floor.

I remember that as a time when I never sat still. I was on my feet all day, directing the workmen as they installed the fixtures and delivered the furniture. There were men who molded the plaster cupids and flowers on the ceilings, welders who installed the brass. The kitchen had been completed first and we ate at a splintery pine table there until the big walnut one arrived.

After working all day, I bathed and changed and worked most of the night — greeting customers, making sure the resort ran smoothly, supervising the girls. After a day when my attention ricochetted from one thing to another, I fell into bed and the day whirled through my head again. A tot of brandy helped to send me off to sleep and I looked forward to the time when I could sit quietly in the afternoons.

Besides the work on the house, there were the girls to train and admonish. Belle tried to work, but the baby needed her and we couldn't have the sound of his screams when the customers came. Her baby, puking and screaming, crying and disrupting, reminded me of what I had lost. It seemed I was on a spiral stairway going down, but I knew that eventually it would stop. In the meanwhile, I was distracted and not thinking too clearly and tired, bone tired all the time.

The weather seemed part of that disconnected time— raw, windy rain, then blaring spring sunshine. Cyclone weather when the sky turned liverish-yellow at dusk and storms blew up out of the prairie to blast through the city.

Belle scarcely had two consecutive hours of sleep. I remember it was around my birthday, in early June when she'd been up all night walking the baby down in the kitchen. Finally, the infant slept. Belle put him to bed and fell asleep on the sofa in the west parlor, near an open window. A sudden storm blew in, the sky darkened and in a few minutes wind-lashed rain pounded the streets.

It rained in on Belle, who was so exhausted she slept through the storm. It wasn't until I made my rounds that afternoon that I found her, clothes soaked, still asleep on the sofa.

We got her to bed, cleaned up the water, moved the sofa out. She contracted a severe cold and it developed into a dangerous lung congestion. It was labor for her just to breathe, wheezing with every breathe, and coughing. The baby was sent to a wetnurse.

The johns were good-natured about having to dodge around packing cases and sit on straight chairs. They teased me about how great it would be when it was finished, if ever it were finished. When the carpenter got the huge French plate mirrors in the ballroom up without damage I could breathe again. They were special-ordered from Pittsburgh and cost $5000. Mirrors to double the light and make everything lively. I had to go to my backers for more money, but they handed it over without complaining. I think they wanted the place for their own enjoyment, more than they wanted their investment back. But they got both.

When I finally called the doctor for Belle, he said he could do nothing for her. With good nursing she might recover. I attended her daily. The other girls kept watch in turn, sometimes missing tricks to stay with her. By September she still had not recovered. I finally decided she couldn't get well.

One day I asked, "What is your father's name?"

"I have no father," she replied. She tried to cough but the congestion choked her and I held her as she gasped for air.

"You have a son. Maybe your father would like to know about that."

"That's why he turned me out."

"Well, I know you're from Knob Noster. How many Watermans can there be?"

"None."

"None?"

She was silent and I could press her no further. Each breath took so much out of her that she could barely speak. I wiped her face and smoothed a little glycerin on her cracked lips. I brushed her long hair out on the pillow, trying not to pull. Then she slept and I sat watching the shadows move around the room as the sun crossed the sky.

Afer an hour her eyes opened. When she saw I was still there, she said, "Emil Peterson. May he burn in hell." And she said no more that day.

I wrote to her father, telling him that his daughter was dying at my place. This is what he wrote back:

My wife is not feeling well and I am so busy with the crops just now that I find that I can't come to Kansas City at this time. If she dies, mark her grave so that we can find it when we find time to come.

Poor Belle hung on until November when she quit breathing. She lay still and pale. When my doctor called he said she was dead. We fixed her, bathed her and dressed her for the grave. There was little embalming in those days. We tied her feet together and she was left on the bed in which she died until her funeral the next day.

I went up and looked at the body several times and then I sent word to the doctor that I just couldn't believe she was dead. She was still, but didn't have that grey cast to the skin. The delicate molding of her face seemed still touched with color. Her thick blond hair was full of glints. The complete relaxation that seems to distort the face of a corpse was missing.

I wept at the loss. I wished she hadn't come and wished I had never become fond. I hated that the rest of us would have to go on without her.

The doctor arrived and became angry. "When I say a person is dead, there is no doubt of it," he stormed.

"Let's put off the funeral for a few days," I begged. "The room is cool and there's no harm."

"Tomorrow," he said and left.

Later that day the Negro maid was cleaning up the rooms on the second floor and I heard a shout of terror where I was downstairs working. I ran up the back stairs to see the maid running down the hallway. She looked as if someone had thrown a handful of flour in her face. If a black woman could ever be described as white, she was white. I grabbed her and held her. She was shaking so I thought she'd collapse.

"What is it, Liza?"

She couldn't say a word, only motioned down the hall toward Belle's room. When I went in I saw that someone had turned the body over. I stood there a moment, trying to think what might have happened. At first I was angry that someone had tampered with the body. After all those weeks, I felt close to this poor girl and wanted no more harm for her. Then it was my turn to take fright. I saw a movement, heard a groan, saw the girl struggle in her shroud. I ripped it open and untied her hands and feet. She groaned some more and began to thrash around. I called the physician back and he helped us revive her. I bit my tongue not to say anything.

From then on, she recovered. She sent the baby to a married sister and by Christmas was turning seven or eight tricks on a good night. Her good looks returned, of course. She was always a cheerful girl and I wondered if her brush with death had made her appreciate the life she had. She was one of the most popular girls in the place.

1874

The life in a bordello was closed, but protected. The prostitutes did not have to risk the dangers of street-walking or give all their money to pimps if they were inmates in a house. Room and board were provided and in some houses, the food and drink were the best. All the girls had to buy were cosmetics and clothes, especially lingerie. If they drank, that took money. Some gave their earnings to boyfriends. Some sent it to family members who needed it. But if a girl was hard-working and saved her money, she could leave the bordello before she lost her looks and strike out on her own. I would be safe in saying that half of my girls married and became good wives. Others sank lower or disappeared. Still others went back home and rejoined their families. A few more went west and opened their own resorts in the raw cattle towns and railheads.

Girls came to me for many reasons. Some already in The Life sought me out and begged to work in a high class house. Some girls had been wronged by some man and cast out from home. It was either a place like this or suicide for them. So I let them in. And then again, there were girls attracted to this Life because they were too lazy for anything else. They didn't want to work for a living, preferring to lie in bed until noon. They came because they could only make the barest subsistence working long hours as shopgirls or in factories and they wanted more than that.

Girls in dressmaking and millinery were in a peculiar bind because their work was always seasonal, with most of their business in the fall and spring. A company that might employ 500 girls at the peak of the season would lay off all but 100 during the slack time. Some of these girls came from small towns and worked long enough to pick up the new styles to take back to their country clients. Others might come from farms and small towns thinking they had secure employment, only to find themselves out of work after three months.

If they came to me I learned that sometimes a hot meal and a loan for train fare home took care of things. I'd find a money order in the mail months later from some small town in Kansas or Iowa or Missouri with a note of thanks.

Sometimes they had nothing to go back to. Kate Sedgewick arrived on my doorstep one cold December day and asked to be admitted to my house. I tried to dissuade her, as I had tried with Belle Waterman. Belle had been with me several years, I think, so this would have been around 1875 or 76.

"Miss Annie, I worked for Robinson's Hats from September to November for $6.50 a week. I couldn't live on that, hardly, staying in a boarding house. There was barely enough for laundry and carfare after I paid the landlady. I didn't have anything put by before I was laid off."

Kate wasn't her real name but the one she took when the girls noticed her Irish sea-green eyes and turned-up nose. That morning her face was pink from the cold.

"Can't you go home?" I asked.

"No home to go to, anymore. I'm clean out of money and if you don't let me come here, I don't know what I'm going to do."

"What have you tried so far?"

"I tried waitressing, but I couldn't work all day on my feet for just $4 a week. Then the manager didn't like me because I wouldn't go in the linen room with him alone, and he got rid of me when he found someone who'd work for $3 a week, the fool. Then I tried finding men on my own."

"What happened?"

"A man named Rabbit Kohler told me I'd have to give what I earned to him and he'd take care of me. I can take care of myself, give me half a chance, and I could see what he was up to. His girls were the sorriest pair of frails I ever laid eyes on, like two whipped bitches. He said if I found johns in his territory, he'd beat me up. That was enough for me." She started crying then, and it wasn't just put on. "If you don't take me, Miss Annie, I'll throw myself off the Hannibal Bridge or take strychnine."

Even though she had free-lanced, her green eyes got big and she chewed her lower lip when I explained about skinning them back and the rest of the routine. She was so dragged out, I told her to rest a day, but that there was no slacking or taking days off after that when it wasn't her period. She perked up after a good night's sleep and a few meals.

Kate was superstitious about the least thing and worried the cook to get rid of a black mouser that reigned in the cellar. She made up for it, though, with dogs. A stray couldn't walk past my door but Kate had it inside, feeding it and petting it. She never talked about her family, but I thought she might have been accustomed to brothers and sisters and the strays took their place. All the girls had a soft spot for animals and sometimes I thought there were more dogs than people in the house.

When I had trouble with girls it was because they had too much time. They slept till noon, got up and ate, then had nothing to occupy them until dinner and evening. I had accounts, orders, inventory, all the details of running a resort that was practically a hotel and restaurant.

They would sit around and sew or read or write letters or sometimes paint or practice music on the piano. If I could have found a way to keep them occupied, there would have been less trouble. When the 1903 flood covered the West Bottoms, we turned the house into a refuge and hospital until all the floor space was filled with pallets and blanketed with sleeping or sick people. The girls and I worked twenty hours a day until everybody was fed and dry, then we kept it up until people could go back and clean up. I had no trouble with boozing, drugs or pimps during those weeks.

But, of course, you can't treat grown women as though they were children in the schoolroom and give them exercises to keep them occupied.

I was in the dining room taking a cup of tea one afternoon. Several girls sat around the big table—probably Belle and maybe Clara Lee, Maude Summers and Big Mary. Big Mary was not grotesque in any way, but simply a full-fleshed woman like me and the other Mary in the house at the time, Little Mary, was a pocket Venus—a 5/8ths scale model woman perfectly proportioned, only smaller than the average. Like as not, if it were a typical day, Little Mary was teaching her schnauzer tricks, using balls of bread to reward the dog. Big Mary was probably sewing up a dress or wrapper. She liked to make them roomy, make herself look as big as possible. There was always some banty rooster of a john who didn't come up to her elbow who wanted a big woman. Belle might have been reading some long romance. She always liked a long story that went on and on, said she got to know the people better when she spent a long time with them. Maybe one girl had folded the tablecloth back and was writing a letter. That would have been about normal. The smell of dinner floated up from the basement and one by one the girls wandered off to bathe and dress. If I had known the arguments over who got to use the tubs and whose turn it was, I would have put in a dozen. But usually they worked out a schedule among themselves.

Then Kate flew in from a trip uptown, breathless and agitated.

"Miss Annie, we've got to close up the house tonight!" she declared as she pulled off her gloves. Then her voice fell to a trembling whisper: "It's too dangerous."

"Close up your honey hole and call yourself a virgin before that would happen," said Big Mary. The others laughed. Little Mary picked up her dog and stroked it as it lay on her lap.

"What are you talking about?" I asked.

"That Kate, she's been to the fortune teller, again," Clara said. Clara believed in johns with feet of clay and her mother's saintliness and not much more.

"Mrs. Marks saw a huge light in her glass, hanging in the sky," said Kate, still breathless. "Then there was a rainfall of either diamonds or ice, like hail. And after that a huge storm blew the light away and all the diamonds and left the grass bare, with no trees. Then a locomotive came running through the grass. Only there were no rails! And after that, the pictures faded."

"What does all that silliness mean, Kate?" asked Maude, who had stopped writing her letter to listen.

"Mrs. Marks says it's in the stars that bad times are coming for somebody close to me, but I will escape. It isn't for me. I want you to close the house, Miss Annie, for your own protection."

"Have a nice cup of tea, Kate, and calm down," I said. "I can't close up every time somebody gets a notion."

"Better not, Miss Annie, we'd all be in sad shape," said Big Mary. "Unless the governor is coming. His assistants are randy as a house full of monkeys. I can't keep up with those hooligans."

"That fortune teller is nothing but a trickster who's

found a way to separate you from your greenbacks," said Maude.

"But something terrible is going to happen!" wailed Kate and then she ran upstairs in tears.

I didn't have much patience with Kate. There were times when one girl or another accused me of playing favorites and I readily admitted I did. I can't help liking some people better than others—men, women or darkies. I tried to administer my rules evenly, though. If the girl was a worker, I didn't have to like her.

But Kate was flighty and I suspected she was taking cocaine or something like that. It was all legal then, just order it from the drug store.

I didn't have much patience with Kate's superstitions. She hung charms on her dresser mirror and dried herbs in her closet. She studied dream books. If she had been Catholic, it would have been what the priest said and candles and saints on her walls. She needed to believe in something, and ended up believing in everything. When the predictions didn't pan out, she was never discouraged. She waited until her next visit, then she'd present us with the newest declaration.

Rosa Marks, the palm reader cum fortune teller, claimed to be a gypsy. Kate walked around the cliff, up to the top of the bluff, then halfway down the rickety wooden steps to Rose Marks' house which looked ready to fall off the side of the West Bluffs. It took her a couple of hours and no streetcars stopped halfway up that steep cliff. I know the Marks woman took money, but I wasn't sure what she scared Kate with to get it.

Kate came down to dinner, dressed to go to work, but unconvinced.

"It's too dangerous today," she said. "The moon and stars are lined up and something terrible will happen, I just know it. Mrs. Marks predicted a bad spell, starting today."

"My ledger predicts a bad time if we don't open," I said.

"You can take the night off, if you're scared, but don't go spreading your black words to the other girls."

"You're not going to open?"

"With you or without you."

She wasn't one of my best girls, so I didn't mind so much if she wasn't downstairs, but I didn't like to be soft with the girls or they'd take advantage. Coming to me the way she did, after being laid off by the milliner and threatened by the pimp, I always had the feeling she wasn't cut out for The Life. She turned tricks well enough, but there was always a touch of distaste, something about the way she held her mouth, that showed she didn't approve. Taking drugs was one way to make it easier. She wouldn't do anything out of the ordinary and more than once I had soothed a john who wanted French or whips. Val and I stopped any really dangerous stuff and the girls could always refuse a john for any good reason. But Kate took advantage of this more than any of the others.

She had a couple of semi-regulars who liked her spooky sayings and the charms. She had no breasts to speak of, but was very trim and graceful, slim for the times.

Something did happen that night, but it was just part of The Life.

It was along about ten, when things were beginning to hum, when I greeted a steady stream of customers and tried to make sure everybody was having a good time. Thurmond Chester came stomping down the stairs with his galluses hanging loose. Now no man would show his galluses in public, and especially somebody as respectable as the treasurer of the livestock commission.

"That chippie has taken my money," he bellowed. I led him off to my wine parlor and nodded to my housekeeper to take over.

"Now calm down, Bubba, and tell me what happened." I poured him a hefty cognac from my private stock. "You went upstairs with, which one was it?"

"Damned scalawag, So . . . So . . . "

"Solange."

"That's the one. Cain't hardly understand that Cajun patter she throws at you."

"What happened?" I sipped my drink.

"Well, you run a first class place here, no hustling the men in and out. So after, uh, we finished, I dozed off. While I was asleep she went through my pocket book and when I went to get dressed, it was lighter by $200."

"When you've finished your drink, we'll get to the bottom of this."

I sent Bubba back to Solange's room and told Val Hayes to get her. She was already back in the ballroom, acting as cool as could be. I had an idea what happened.

"Girl, give this man back the money."

"Madame, I swear, I do not have it. I take no money."

"It's gone and I've known Bubba longer than I've known you."

I took her to her room and walked over to the barred window and looked around. She was cool, I'll give her that. But I found what I was looking for—a spool of heavy button thread tucked between the cushion and the arm of the easy chair. I heard her gasp.

"Tell me," I said.

"I tell nothing!" she screamed. She ran toward Bubba and threw herself on him. "Please, m'sieur, I do nothing!"

Val pulled her off.

"You didn't tell me you had a pimp who followed you up here from New Orleans," I accused. "Roll the john and lower the money through the bars to your man. Where is he staying?"

She went sullen then and refused to say anything.

"Pack your things and be out of here by morning," I said. "Clear out while Bubba gets dressed."

I turned on my heel and left. Val watched her in the hall and when Bubba came down, galluses neatly covered by his coat, we had another drink. I had $200 from my safe ready for him.

Val told me later he watched her pack, then took her trunk down the back stairs. She followed in a few minutes. He flagged a hack and she took off. He didn't catch the name of the hotel. Bubba was pacified and the rest of the evening went smoothly.

The next morning, I discovered Solange's revenge. She had thrown the contents of her chamber pot wholesale all over the room. Stinking stains covered the bed and bed-clothes, the wallpaper, the carpet, the upholstered chair — every place they could do the most damage. The smell was awful and I could see the room would have to be stripped to the plaster. Liza called in a friend, Polly Walker, who helped her clean up. Polly was a good worker and I kept her on. The two maids got along and business was good. No need to work Liza so hard she quit. That $200 ended up costing me many more hundreds before it was over. Bubba never brought it up, but I know word got out that I played fair.

As I held a hanky to my nose and looked at the damage Solange had inflicted, I remembered Kate's gypsy's predic-tion. Well, having to dismiss a girl wasn't unusual. If it wasn't for stealing (or cheating on the house), it was drink-ing or drugs. I examined the girls regularly, but if a girl took the clap she was out. First, I taught them how to squeeze the customer to make sure there was nothing dis-eased, then I taught them how to do it with finesse. Some-times a girl would put herself out of The Life. Brides and whores sometimes get terrible infections, some disease where they can't pee and they're in pain all the time. They can't work and there's nothing for it but to quit. Fighting and jealousies and minor squabbles were usual, but knives or firearms meant the girl was out.

I had just put Liza and Polly to work that morning when I was called downstairs to talk to a politician. This was

before the Pendergasts got their grip on the North End. I
invited the first ward alderman into my wine parlor.

"Elections are coming up in a few months, Miss Annie,"
he said. He was a big man with a belly that supported a
lengthy gold watch chain. My mama said a politician was
like a cat: they're friendly when they want something, but
when they get it, they disappear.

"What does the election mean to me?" I asked.

"I could use a little support from the people in my ward,
for expenses associated with elections."

He was being very careful. It wasn't blackmail; it
wouldn't be a bribe. It would be an anonymous gift.

"I've been happy with the way you've represented us," I
said. "No reason you shouldn't get elected again. What
kind of help do you need?"

"About $500 should carry me through, pay for workers,
printed materials and cover the cost of rallies and such."

I wondered how much "such" he was planning. That
was enough to pay for three campaigns. His rallies
included free lunch and a good-sized keg. Sometimes his
people got rowdy when they paraded, but nothing Speers'
men couldn't handle.

"I'm a little short right now," I admitted. "But I could
probably help you out before the election heats up. Can
you wait a few weeks?"

He didn't look pleased. He pulled at the ends of his
mustache and frowned. "Well, if you ain't got it, you ain't
got it. But you do a big business here and I thought, well,
I thought you'd like to do a friend a good turn."

"No doubt about that, Goody. But it takes money to
make money. I'll see there's a contribution to your cam-
paign coming soon."

The house had been paid off but there were operating
expenses and wages to be paid. It wasn't as bad as '74, the
year of the Panic. I sat down with my books and worked
out where to dig up the $500. Later I worked out a similar

arrangement with the Pendergasts. We operated like rail-road tracks—side by side in the same place, but never crossing each other. The brothers wanted power and a little madam like me wasn't of interest to them. Having my prosperous friends meant things were easier for me than they might have been. No minor official was going to try any reform when people higher up might be burned. Later, there was no stopping the reform. The prohibition-ists and anti-vice people and the rest drove honest whores and saloonkeepers out of business. I wondered about the gypsy's prediction.

The following night Kate was persuaded to come out of her room and join the rest of the girls. She acted flighty, popping out of her chair at the least distraction and I wondered if she had taken enough morphine or cocaine to get hopped up. That night a man in a muddy greatcoat arrived late. He seemed to be drunk, but not falling-down stupid. More of a feverish kind of drunk. He called for girls and champagne and paid with a lavish hand. He danced for a while, whirling and shouting until he wore out one partner, then another. I signalled Val to keep his eye on this one.

The john went upstairs for an all-night session with Kate. The two of them were wild as March hares—her with her starts and him with whatever put a burr under his saddle. I waited to see if there was any sign of trouble from Kate's room, but all seemed normal and I told Val to go to bed then went to mine.

I awoke as usual and threw on a dressing gown to go to the kitchen for coffee. There was the usual morning-after stink of cigar smoke and stale booze, the closed-in smell of chamber pots, sex, sweat and human bodies. The maids would air when they cleaned. The heavy draperies shut out the sunshine and in the shadowy main parlor something was awry. Then I saw by the scuff marks in the carpet and the scratches on the oak floor that the big circular settee had been pushed into the ballroom. Swinging from the big chandelier was Kate's trick, hanging by his suspenders. I tore open the draperies for more light. He had pushed the settee under the gas fixture, put a chair on top of the pedestal back and looped his braces over the arm of the chandelier. Then he'd kicked the chair away. It lay on its back a few feet from the settee.

I stood there, trying to take a deep breath and calm down before I called for help. His tongue stuck out of his discolored face. I don't know why I was so sure who it was—he was barely recognizable. His shirt and trousers were loose as doll clothes. He turned a little to one side, then a little to the other. The mirrors of the ballroom reflected his feet and legs, hanging like some frightful bait into the mirrored bowl of the room.

I stared for a minute more, then called Val and sent him to the police station. While the police were taking the man down I remembered Kate. I went to her room and woke her up. I shouted something at her, but she must have known nothing. When I dragged her down to the ball-room in her wrapper, she took one look at the dangling body and fainted.

The policeman in charge did his job and they soon had the man out of the place. It was suicide simple enough and Ned Stewart saw that there were no problems. There was another time when a wholesale contractor died of apoplexy in bed with a girl. It took some doing to get him into a room at the Pacific House where his family could find him with no scandal.

When the smelling salts finally brought Kate around I pulled her into a chair and sat down opposite her.

"Look at me, girl, and if you lie I'll know it. Did you say anything to that wild jasper last night about your moon and stars?"

"No, no," she said immediately. I waited. She hadn't taken time to think before she spoke. I held her by the wrist and looked straight at her.

"Well, he asked me what the stuff on my mirror was and I told him," she said. "He seemed to think they were funny or something, so I clammed up. All I can remember is that he said something about needing more than a charm. He paid for the night, but he must've slipped out after I fell asleep."

The police found out the suicide had been in bad money trouble and had lost his business, then his wife left him. He spent the last money he had on a spree at my house, then ended it. What could make a man lose all hope? As bad as things had been when I lost my babes and Willie or when I told Richmond to leave, I could never directly kill myself. There was some streak of stubbornness or something that kept me going. Maybe I was too mean to die until I got mine back on the world. I always wondered about that john and what kind of setback would make one man more determined to succeed and send the other to a sporting house to end it.

I got goosebumps thinking about the gypsy's prediction and I was glad when Kate packed up and left for Chicago later that year. I did miss her dogs, though.

Some girls like Kate Sedgewick weren't cut out for The Life. They forced themselves into it and sometimes it worked and sometimes not. Others came into The Life with a more straightforward attitude and some even had a talent for it. One girl who seemed to take to it naturally was Nellie Tobias. She had drifted into The Life and found her talents were appreciated.

She told me this story afterward, parts of it. Of course, I knew her and saw most of it happening. It was such a singular story that I've never forgotten it. It was early on— must have been New year's Day of '74 or '75.

Shelby Gustaffson woke up in Nellie's room that New Year's Day. He'd lost his cherry, all his money gambling and the skin off his knees on Nellie's sheets. He leaped out of bed and lost everything he'd eaten the day before into the washbasin. She clambered after him and held his head.

"Shit fire and fox manure."

"What?"

"I never felt so good and so bad at the same time." He checked the pocket of his waistcoat to see if he still had his return ticket on the Santa Fe to Dodge City. It was there and he turned his other pockets out, hoping he had missed a dime or two bits. Clean broke.

By this time Nellie was sitting back on the bed with the sheets and quilts tumbled around her, hair in points, her face shiny. She yawned and watched Shelby towel his lantern-jawed face and rub his carrot hair. He looked mild, almost simple, because of his prairie blue eyes with rabbity white lashes, but he was all sinew under the freckles which speckled everywhere the sun had reached.

"What're you talking about?" she asked. She tended to be grumpy in the mornings. She had come to me from a resort in Harlem across the river right after I opened my big house. She was not the prettiest girl in the place, but she might have been the smartest. She knew her business right enough and made no bones about it. I always think of a ripe peach when I think of Nellie. Her smooth skin had the yellow-pink glow of a peach blush and her hair was dark as the bark of a peach tree. She was tiny, barely came up to Shel's shoulders and she looked as soft as a ripe peach, but that was deceptive.

I had noticed them the night before, laughing together like they hit it off well.

"Here I am, I never felt worse in my life and I'm still saying I love you." He put his breeches on over his longhandles and started buttoning his shirt. "You're bad tempered and you're going to get fat laying around this whorehouse, but you're smart and you're funny, least you was last night, and you ain't lazy, if you take a mind to do something. I could tell that right off."

"I'm supposed to run off with you when you just told me you want to marry me and you're broke and I'm the first and only woman you ever been with? You're tetched."

She went to the door and hollered, "Polly!" When the black maid came she said, "Clear away this mess and bring me some hot water. And take that washstand stuff, too.

Open that window," she commanded Shel, "or I'm going to be sick, too."

"It's New Year's Day and you want the window open?"

"It stinks in here."

Shel pulled on his jacket, then raised the sash. The damp, piercing air from the river rushed into the room. Nellie shivered, satisfied, and pulled off her wrapper.

"How'm I going to make you believe me?" Shel asked. "I want to marry you and go back and start a farm and a family and be like a normal person."

"I say you're full of it."

When Polly brought the water Nellie lowered the window then began to wash.

He waited and she soaped her face and neck with a flannel rag.

"You bring me two pieces of paper, no three," she said going on to her breasts and armpits. "One, I want to see the deed to any farm and how much is owed. Two, I want to know you got some money in some bank. About $500 minimum. And three," she said as she handed Shel the rag to scrub her back, "I want a signed statement from you with witnesses and notarized seals and everything that you will never mention out loud to a soul—to anybody, not to me, not to children, strangers nor family, that you found me in a whore house."

She bent to her task, then looked up through tousled dark hair that had fallen in her face to see how he took it. He looked stunned.

"Them's your terms?" he said.

"Take it or leave it."

"You mind me asking a couple of questions?"

"Ask."

"Why the deed?"

"I want to know I'm going to something that ain't going to kill me. My mama died of the cholera, they said, but I watched her try to keep that farm going after Daddy passed on and I think she worked herself to death. If something happens to you I want the farm free and clear and all mine to sell so's I don't have to work myself to death."

"Well, I can see how that's prolly a good idea. Why so much money in the bank? That's a lot for a buffalo skinner to save up, while he's finding a place to farm."

"In case something goes wrong. If we're going to have kids, we got to be prepared for their sakes. Besides, everything always takes more money than you plan."

"And that signed statement," he continued. "If you're ashamed of being a frail, why'n't you cook or be a maid or something. You don't have to do this."

"I do if I want to make more than just the bare minimum to live. Don't tell me about housemaiding. It's twelve hours a day and you can't make enough to buy yourself a dresslength but once a year." She soaped her nether regions. "Besides, I ain't ashamed of what I do. I do it better than any girl here. But I ain't going off to Lonesome, Kansas, and have all the sanctimonious wives treat my kids bad because they found out about me. I can face down any man or woman around, but it ain't fair to put little kids through that." She paused to rinse. "And I ain't going to have you throw it up to me ever time you get mad and ask questions. How many men and what did I do different with them I don't do with you and how much money and who and all that. Now you think about it and tell me you want to marry me." She dried her feet.

"I want to marry you."

She looked up, surprised.

"You're the funniest man on two legs I ever been with," she said. She pulled drawers and corset cover out and sat on the bed to dress. "You're a loving fool and seem smart enough, except for wanting to marry a whore. And not bad looking—you're all wiry muscle, what there is of you."

Shel stood with his shoulders thrown back and his belly

sucked flat, listened and grinned. Nellie grabbed clothes out of a chiffionier.

"I'd take a chance on you just for fun. But you're talking about farming and marrying and kids. How do I know you won't fade after a few months, leave me stranded? How do I know you don't drink? How do I know you don't take up with ever gal that comes along? How do I know you got good sense? Well?"

"Hunh?" Shel had been watching cotton lisle stockings and ruffled underskirts cover the rosy skin. Then she handed him a dress of sprigged muslin to hold while she slipped it over her head. He hadn't been paying strict attention.

"Oh, hell." Nellie opened the door and hollered for the maid again. She ordered eggs, biscuits, sausage, gravy and coffee downstairs.

"I cain't pay for it. Told you I was broke."

"I'll stake you to breakfast," said Nellie. "Least I can do for my future husband." Her voice was dry with doubt when she told me about that conversation, one side of her mouth twisted up and the other down as if she tried to be cynical but couldn't help smiling.

"You feel OK to eat?" she asked.

"I think so." Shel had trouble concentrating. She brushed her dark hair into smooth waves and tied it back with a lavender ribbon. She led him downstairs to the dining room where they sat alone at the end of the long table.

I came through about then and Nellie introduced us. I wondered about her giving breakfast to a trick, but I figured she knew what she was doing.

Nellie made him repeat her terms until he could recite them back, then she said: "I know I'm steady and I can take care of myself."

"On your back," he grumbled.

"Wherever. I've made enough trips up those stairs I bet I could climb Pike's Peak and never get winded. Now I want to see how steady you are. What does a buffalo skinner do?"

"He finds a buffalo runner, the one who shoots, and hooks up with him. The runner, he gets the wagons and supplies, and we go out until he finds some buffs. Then he shoots them and we skin them. When the wagons are full, we go back to the railhead and split the take, except for expenses."

"I've talked to some hunters, but not any skinners."

"Not many's as good as me, nor as fast. And I'm careful with my money, usually. Never played that faro game before." He grinned at her.

"I think I love you, Shelby," admitted Nellie. "As much as I want to throw myself in your arms and run off to Kansas, I can't."

"You ain't dumb and it's only fair I earn what I want. And that's you." He leaned across the table and kissed her cheek. "Promise you'll wait."

"I'll be here or leave word where I'm at with Miss Annie." Nellie took Shel's hand and smoothed the calluses and scars with her cool fingers. "When you coming back?"

"This is New Year's. If you don't see me by the Fourth of July, you can give up on me."

"Good," she said and they clasped hands.

Then Nellie remembered herself and sat back down at the table, all business.

"Will you write me?" she asked.

"Don't put much store by it."

"You *can* write?"

"Yes," he said patiently. "And figger and know when to go to court, if I need to. My daddy was a conscientious man."

"I'll bide my time, then."

"There's no place you can mail a letter to. I'll be out working. Wright's in Dodge might hold letters for me, but I don't count on it. I'd write you love poems, if I could,"

"I won't count on that, either."

"You ain't very sentimental," he complained.

"You got enough for both of us," she replied. She told me later that she talked tough partly because she was try- ing to cover up being scared. He looked at her and she thought he understood that.

"Tell me about your family," she said, more composed. "If I'm going to be related to them I need to know. What kind of man was your daddy?"

"What kind was yours?"

"Just a dirt farmer."

"Where abouts?"

"Otterville."

"Never heard of it."

"Near Sedalia."

"What kind of farm?"

"I don't recollect. Before the war I was too little, and after it was just my Mama and sometimes hired help and it was corn and cows, as long as we had them."

"How old are you?"

"How old are you?" she countered.

"Tell me how old you are and I'll tell about my daddy."

"Eighteen. And last night you were twenty-one. I remember now."

"Yes," said Shel. "Well, my daddy used to be a farmer, too. Till he decided to go in with his cousin. They were going to run this store. But the store went bust and daddy lost all his money. His cousin had more money to begin with so he's still a farmer and daddy's working for a man down in the bottoms who's got a feed mill. Daddy comes home covered with grain dust. Thinks he's still a gentle- man and shouldn't get dust on his clothes. Moans all the time about losing the farm. All he's got is a money name. Got no money any more."

"How come you didn't stay here abouts? Your uncle'd have pull."

"Couldn't stand all the pissing and moaning over

money. Decided I'd go make my own. Start fresh. I came back for Christmas and it's still the same. Complaining about money. Talking about who married whose cousin and who ain't speaking to who and whether Aunt Billie's baby came too soon after the wedding and who owes money and I got plum full of that stuff. So I went out and blew all I had last night. I'll start again as soon as I get back, find a runner to skin for. This time I'll have something to look forward to."

I couldn't have been more surprised if Nellie had grown feathers and crowed. But I sent for my lawyer, Ned Stewart, and he drew up the papers that day. I witnessed and signed and Ned put his seal on those strange contracts.

Shel and Nellie spent the rest of the day in her room, then he caught the Santa Fe for Dodge and she came back after seeing him off at the depot.

"Miss Annie, I want to quit hooking."

"You're my best girl," I said, surprised. I had thought she had her head on straight.

"I know. But there are plenty of girls. Let me be housekeeper here. You're working yourself silly trying to do everything. I know mostly how things go and what I don't know you can tell me and you'll only have to tell me once. I give myself until the Fourth of July, same as I gave him. I never promised I wouldn't turn tricks, but I want to stop now. What do you say?

"Let me think about it. Will you work tonight?"

"I'm beat from today with Shelby."

"You go along and I'll let you know tomorrow."

I could have kicked Nellie out, but she had always been straight with me. She'd turn eight or ten tricks on a good night and never complain. I had nearly a full complement, fifteen girls and two more Creoles coming from New Orleans, so I couldn't say I was shorthanded. Still, I hated to lose a good worker.

I had the feeling that she had made a private contract to match the ones Shel had signed.

And she was right about my needing help. I got up and checked accounts, ordered food, bought supplies, checked the maid's work, made sure the girls were in good health. One laundress had quit and I'd ended up buying new sheets so we wouldn't run out. You've got to have food, and the better the food, the happier the girls and the customers. Clean goes without saying and there were plenty of black maids. The cook and the houseman, Dora and Val, were steady and I provided their living quarters separate from the rest. But there was always a problem with laundry. I know it's back-breaking work, but someone's got to do it. But laundresses get pregnant or they get drunk or they get the vapors or the tubs tip over and they get down in the back. I must have had an army of laundresses over the years. Commercial laundries came along but not until it was almost too late for me.

I decided I could use some help and Nellie and I decided on a wage. It was much less than she could've made turning tricks, but she seemed satisfied and I thought she was worth a try.

A couple of months went by and it all worked out. Nellie took care of the little details like laundry and whether the wainscotting needed polish and how to get the prisms on the chandelier clean and which girl needed to replace lingerie and who was hitting the laudanum. I had time to deal with tradesfolk and plan ahead. Some weekends I had $10,000 in my safe, but expenses ran high, too. Besides my backers to pay, there were bills for upkeep and replacement. Sometimes I had to send a chair out for reupholstery before it was paid for. Nellie was a big help.

Then one day she came into the office where I was checking accounts.

"Miss Annie, I think I'm pregnant."

"You certain?"

"I've always been regular as a clock. Been two months."

"Why did you wait so long? When you're late, there's ways to bring you around."

"I know." She looked down and seemed to want to tell me something. It took a few minutes to sink in, then I realized she didn't want to get rid of it. Most whores automatically take care of that problem as one of the risks of the job. They know about douching and how to pack themselves with a sponge soaked in vinegar. There was always pennyroyal if she couldn't "fall off the roof." Or the black pill and hot baths.

"You think it's Shel's baby?" I asked.

She nodded. "Pretty sure."

"And you want to keep it?"

"Yes."

"You trust that crazy cowboy to come back, then?"

"Always hoped he would."

"Well, I wouldn't count on it. But if this is what you want to do, it won't change anything. You can do your work as housekeeper pregnant—that won't change. You have money put by?"

"Yes. Been putting some back a little at a time since New Year's too."

"Well, you can stay here and there's no problem, but I was thinking about expenses."

"I think I'll have plenty."

She'd worked this out and seemed glad when I went along with it. In for a penny, in for a pound. She was a good girl and a smart worker. She looked relieved. I got up and gave her a hug and told her to take it easy if she felt bad and that it would all work out. She left smiling.

I didn't think that crazy Shel would come back, but I didn't want to burden her with my doubts.

1875

After the hard year of 1874, things started to settle down. The grasshopper invasion stripped the Kansas plains and Congress passed laws saying homesteaders could be absent from their lands to look for work.

The effects of the financial panic of '73 were wearing off. The country survived the scandals of Grant's administration. The banks in town had even closed and the stocks and gold prices went crazy. They did get the waterworks going. Speers was named chief of the newly-organized police force. The Centennial Exposition planned for the next year in Philadelphia gave people something to look forward to.

Custer had been to the Black Hills and it took until the Greasy Grass, another year, before he was through. Major Miles was still chasing Comanches and Apaches west into Arizona.

This was the time of the cowboy out west and of long drives to Abilene and Dodge City to ship the cattle to Chicago or here, to Kansas City, where the slaughterhouses received them. Cowboys couldn't afford my prices, but cattlemen from as far away as Texas and Wyoming patronized my place. Barbed wire was patented in '74, but it took a few more years before the effects were felt and more and more open range was fenced.

That winter of '75 gusts of damp river air entered with every customer, the horses' hooves rang on the paving bricks like brass and the trolley bells' chimes hung on the cold air. A few weeks after Nellie broke her news, Bubba sent a message that he was bringing some out-of-town business associates to my establishment. I laid on an especially good dinner of Chateaubriand and creamed vegetables. I bought home-preserved vegetables and fruit when I could. I ordered my best cauliflower and pole beans and a cream cake for desert.

That night the dining table was set with my French china banded in blue and gold. Each Waterford glass sparkled, the silver gleamed against the white damask cloth. Low bowls of hothouse roses added color. They were nearly without scent and would not interfere with the smells of the food.

Early that evening, about eight, Bubba arrived with his party. I recognized Altman and McKinley from the livestock commission, Mort Dively and another banker. It looked as though they might be putting together some investment combination for the out-of-towners.

I stood at the end of the entryway, smiling, greeting those I knew and meeting the visitors from Chicago and other cities.

Polly hung their heavy coats and took their hats, then one of the girls showed them to the dining room.

The last man doffed his coat and turned from the cloakroom to face me.

It was Richmond

I felt the blood drain from my face and I reached for the molding at the doorway. He looked a little older, a little greyer in his black broadcloth suit and cravat, but he might have been coming to me naked, ready to take me down.

"Annie." He moved toward me with urgent grace. My knees buckled and I grasped the molding.

All the bitterness and anger were cold and I felt as though we had never ceased to be lovers.

I stammered something and he saw I was about to fall. He wrapped one arm around my waist and held me while I lifted shaking arms to his neck. He brushed a kiss across my cheek and I could feel the flutter begin inside. I turned to kiss him and felt the strength of his arms. It heartened me and reassured me.

"Come to my room," I whispered and led him to the wine parlor. Once the door was shut, he ran his hands over my body, as if to remind himself. I could not speak, but only stood there, thankful that I could touch him once again.

I pulled his coat off and began twisting the studs out of his stiff shirt. He reached up to cup my breasts and I left his shirt to unbutton my bodice. The clothes of those days were fussy to get on and off.

He stood in his socks laughing while I stood struggled with petticoats. He tried to help and we got tangled in the ties.

"You must be out of practice," he teased.

The dark hair on his chest was thicker. There was a softening in the middle, but his legs were strong as iron and his arms, with their pelt of dark hairs, reached for me. He ran his hands from my face down my breasts, over my belly and thighs to my feet. I shivered from cold and excitement. He knelt and buried his face in my private places and my knees began to give way again.

I raised his head between my hands and tasted myself on his lips. He wrapped his arms around me and supported me as I led him to my big brass bed. We explored those still remembered places, then when we could wait no longer, rolled into the center of that snowy field and joined.

The old responses had slept but not died. I rose at his

touch and stifled my cries with the lace-edged corner of a pillow.

We collapsed, rested, and without a word, began again.

After another rising climax, I fainted or slept. When I came to myself, he was asleep beside me. His well-loved face was relaxed, one arm flung up, legs sprawling where I had not had another's legs in a long time. I curled around him, accommodating myself to his posture, and floated in a half dream.

"Miss Annie, are you all right?" Nellie called through the door.

I slipped out of the bed and went to the outer door.

"Take over for me. I can't come out tonight."

"Are you sick?" She sounded worried.

"No. I just can't be there. See that the group has the best of everything. Please, Nellie."

"Yes, Miss Annie."

Her footsteps faded down the hall.

I tried to slip back between the sheets without disturbing Richmond, but he roused and gave me a sleepy smile as he opened his arms to me again.

Later he sent word to his friends he would not return with them to their hotel. I ordered a late supper before the cook went to bed.

"This was a gift," he said. "Finding you like this. I saw you when you came in and I didn't know how you would take it. You might have cursed and thrown me out. You'd have reason enough after what happened."

"I always loved you."

"I knew that, but I didn't want to know it."

He raised his cup for a last swallow, then wiped his mouth and leaned away from the table.

"How are you . . . ?" I began.

"My family thrives. The big ones have grown and there is another little one. We are happy enough."

I looked into my teacup and said nothing. The family was happy. But his voice was thin and neutral as he spoke.

"I'm glad," I said. "I meant good for your family."

Now he was silent. When he spoke his voice was husky and heavy.

"I have nothing like this. Like you. No fire." He cleared his throat. "We have separate paths now but perhaps we can make them cross again."

I looked at his eyes to see if they told me anything. Their brown corneas, threaded with gold, were quiet as he looked away, somewhere over my shoulder. Then he drew a breath and looked at me and the eyes danced. He told me about his business, about quitting as alderman, about what his company was making now. We laughed at the things he'd tried—a new plow, carriage fittings—that hadn't worked or made money. I filled him in on how I financed the house and how I'd been around the country. I told him the story of the painting and what a bother the mirrors in the ballroom were. He told me about his children—how smart the boys were, how accomplished the girl was. There was a new baby, but I couldn't be jealous that he slept with his wife. I hadn't been celibate, myself.

Sometimes it happens with friends, not even your closest friend, but someone you hit it off with. They leave or you leave and you don't see each other, sometimes for years. But when you get back together, it's as though you pick up right where you left off. It was that way with Belle and with Ambrose Leary, a buffalo runner I'd known in Kentucky. It was that way with Richmond, and we laughed and talked as we ate, stepping on each other's stories, exclaiming at what had happened, enjoying each other's company.

"I'm so happy that we had this chance to remember what we had," I said. I put my teacup down and rose to stand beside him. Then I knelt at his knees and took his face in my hands.

"I can't bear to think that we will never be together." I

began to cry and could feel my face grow hot and crumpled. I would look awful, but I couldn't help it. I put my head on his knee.

He stroked my back until I quieted, then he said: "We cannot live together, but we can meet."

"In secret."

"It's best."

"Yes."

"I travel on business to other cities. Is that too tawdry?"

"No. I will go anywhere you tell me, if I can." I wiped my eyes.

"It may not happen like this often."

"So be it."

That morning he left to join his group of businessmen for their meetings, and came back alone that night. I turned over the house to Nellie, and Richmond and I talked and loved and drank and slept and loved once more before he left.

Spring came all of a sudden that year. It was freezing rain and frost killing the peach blossoms, then it was summer. Sometimes it seems we have no spring, unless you've been watching for the buds on the trees and getting a garden ready. There was no garden behind Third and Wyandotte, and that year it seemed spring flew by in a day or two and hot summer was on us before I noticed.

Nellie started to get big. She had the mask and looked like a fat raccoon sometimes, but she was cheerful and hard working.

She got one short letter from Shelby saying he had found a place he liked, but that the buffalo had been hard to find and he was having trouble with the leader of the party. Then nothing.

July came and went and he didn't show up. That didn't surprise me and I expected Nellie to take it to heart, but she seemed as cheerful as ever. She got big as a barn and could hardly walk. I went to Hot Springs for two weeks during the hottest part of August and when I came back I asked her when she thought she was due.

"Today, if I had my way. But probably not for a few weeks, if my calculations are right."

Toward the end of September she was brought to bed and after a long day and night when none of the other girls could keep their minds on anything else, she produced a great, fat boy. She recovered in a few days and he nursed like a bull calf. We teased her that he was half-grown when he was born and she just laughed. She went back to work in a few weeks as housekeeper and both of them seemed fine and happy. But along toward Christmas I sat down with her by the fire in her room while she nursed that baby and asked her what she was going to do.

"Do you mean, will I stay here as housekeeper?" she asked.

"Yes, or come back to The Life. It's hard to raise a child alone and you'd make more money as one of the girls than you do now."

"I still think Shelby will come back."

"Wanting him back won't make it happen. I don't mean to be cruel, but to find out how to plan," I said. I wondered how she remained steadfast and cheerful with only one letter for reassurance. She might be just keeping a brave face to the world.

"I'll stay your housekeeper for a few months longer," Nellie said, "then I'll have to decide something in the spring if Shelby doesn't come."

It must have been while Nellie waited, that Ned showed up one afternoon and said he wanted to talk to me privately.

I sat him down in the little wine parlor and wondered what he was so serious about. It wasn't like him.

"I could just've not come around and sooner or later you'd hear about it, but that didn't seem right."

I waited and felt my heart grow heavy.

"So I wanted to tell you straight on," he continued. "I'm

getting married." He told me the name of the daughter of a prominent man who had banking and real estate interests.

I roused myself and pasted on a smile. "Let me be the first to congratulate you. She must be a fine girl if you've chosen her."

He dropped his eyes and didn't say anything more.

"She'll never know you've been anything but pure," I said. I thought he might wonder about disease.

"I want to thank you, Annie." His voice was croaky. "It's been great."

"It sure has. And you'll still be my lawyer, I hope."

"Yes." Still he sat with his eyes down.

"What's troubling you?"

"I don't want anything about us to get back to my wife."

"Of course not. I never talk. I'd be out of business if people couldn't trust me."

Then it hit me. *He* had talked about our liaison and was afraid I would, too. That made his news a little heavier to bear, but I had no claims I could make, whatever I felt.

"Don't worry, Ned. Only men who have seen you here will know anything and they're not likely to advertise it."

He seemed relieved and I got him out of there as quickly as I could.

I didn't know I would feel so bad. I had other friends besides Ned. It was just that he had been the first in Kansas City and it reminded me that time was passing.

I had Val fetch a hack right away. I skipped dinner and had the hackman drive me to Westport, where he watered the team, then I told him to keep driving. He drove to Byrum's Ford on the Blue River and on to Independence before I let him turn back. I didn't think; I tried not to feel. I just felt the air moving over my face and the rig jouncing in the ruts and over the car tracks. I felt stony cold and just went ahead and felt bad. I even cried until my hanky was used up. It wasn't the worst I ever felt, but it was bad and I decided that if feeling bad was the price of having lovers, then I'd pay the price and hope the bill didn't come due too often.

The Christmas season grew with parties and fights and merrymaking until the day itself burst and we all were thankful for a few idle days and nights before the New Year holiday.

New Year's Eve was a big night, as always. I had asked the leader of the little orchestra I kept for dancing to hire more musicians. He found three Negro musicians who played piano and banjos and our dancers circled the ballroom to music from one group or the other all night. I instructed the cook to lay out a buffet and have plenty of champagne ready. Many prosperous men made their New Year's call that night, some just to see how the resort was doing, some to take a girl upstairs. The next day they would pay calls on Quality Hill with their proper wives, leaving engraved cards on silver trays. They left no cards with me, but I wagered I could match names with the finest hostesses if all were told.

The next day the house was a shambles. We hadn't put the big chain across the door until nearly dawn and no one was stirring at midmorning except me. The spittoons were filled with tobacco juice and the wallpaper around each one was stained and would need to be replaced. Spilled food and wine covered the ballroom floor and the 20-foot mirror was blotched with splashes and sticky handprints. The West Parlor was a mess from a daisy chain. My slippers stuck to the rugs. They'd have to be taken up for cleaning. The kitchen was nearly bare and all the shops were closed for the holiday. We'd rest and make do with mush and milk for today, I thought, and perhaps close the house for a few days until we could make repairs and clean up. I walked over to turn off the lights in the front hallway. An empty champagne bottle rolled down the last few steps and hit the tiles with a glassy thud.

Just then the doorbell sounded. I tied my wrapper more

tightly around and went to the window. My mouth fell open. Standing there with the soot from the Santa Fe still smudging his face was Shelby Gustaffson.

"Just a minute," I cried and ran for the key. I dragged the heavy chain in and opened the door. I was so glad to see him for Nellie's sake, I threw my arms around him and drew him inside.

"Nellie's room is at the back of the house, down the long hallway," I said. He took off before I could say more. I followed because I wanted to see his face when he saw his son.

"Which room, Miss Annie?" he asked.

I knocked on Nellie's door, pushed it open and Shel looked in, dumbfounded and happy and surprised all at once. I looked over at Nellie. She was smiling, then she was laughing, then he rushed in and knelt down where she was nursing that baby and wrapped his arms around them both. He laid his callused hand on the red fuzz on the baby's head. I closed the door.

I sent the houseman over to the Sheridan Hotel for food to celebrate and waited until the three came downstairs. By that time most of the rest of the girls were stirring. It was a pretty dragged-out bunch, but everybody was glad for Nellie, even the ones who'd complained I'd favored her.

After we had eaten the pick-up meal and opened a few bottles of champagne that had been missed, Shelby told us what happened:

"First, I hooked up with a hunter who had a good reputation. But he drank. When he went to set up his shooting sticks his hand shook so bad he had to call one of the skinners to help him. He started shooting and the shaggies scattered before he'd dropped a dozen. We only had a day's skinning amongst us. That was the way it went—a day late and a dollar short. Never could find the big herds."

Shel held Nellie's hand, and did not drop it even when he gestured.

"Then I joined up with another crew, this time two old hands who knew their way around. After we'd sold a few loads and I was starting to fill up my pocketbook, I took some time off and scouted for a farm. Seemed like all the good places were already taken, but I found a claim one man had given up and I got it. He had a cabin and there was water, but Indians had scared his wife too many times."

I stole a glance at Nellie but she showed no sign at the mention of Indians. I'd heard too many stories from cavalry officers not to take them seriously. Compared to the luxury of the resort, it would be a harsh and perhaps dangerous life, but it would be hers.

"I figured a couple of hunts," said Shelby, "and I'd pay it off easy. So I found another outfit and we went after the buffs again. This time we had to travel even further to find them. They're getting scarcer ever time. The next bunch got ruint when a herd stampeded and ran right over the staked out hides and tore them to bits. Then the runner and a couple of his old buddies took off with the wagons and left us with just our warbags and ponies. Took us, there was three of us, a long time to get back to town. First one thing, then another."

Nelly patted his arm and smiled at him.

"I got the farm paid off," he continued, "and put in some time working on the cabin. It ain't much, but it's a real wood cabin with a stone foundation and root cellar, not a soddie. The man I bought it from had done a right smart bit of work on it before he gave it up.

"After that I went out skinning again and I was a hundred miles from a post office on the Fourth of July, Nellie, and that's the truth. We even went down into Comanche country in October looking for buffs and about the middle of November a blue norther came up and we almost froze waiting it out. That country is flat as a griddle with noth-

ing to break the wind but a few rocks and maybe a cotton-
wood tree. When I got back to Dodge it was hard winter
already. I had just $489 in my pocket. I decided if I went
out again I'd use up the last of my luck, bad as it'd been,
so I took a chance that Nellie'd still be waiting and take me
even if I was a few greenbacks short."

Then he turned and hugged Nellie and the baby again.

Nellie spent some of that money on things she thought
she'd need in the cabin. She left the baby one day long
enough to meet Shelby's family who didn't take to her at
all. They got married at City Hall and came back for a
luncheon where the girls showered her and the baby with
enough clothes and diapers and wrappers for a dozen
babies. Nellie said that's how many she aimed to have, so
nothing would go to waste. Then we loaded everything
that wasn't already shipped into a hack and they took off
for the depot.

Every year on the Fourth of July I'd get a letter from
Nellie, bringing me up to date. She didn't have a dozen
children, but quit after six. She joined the church, Presbyterian I think, and the Sewing Circle and later, the Tem-
perance League. They were as happy as two people could
be. He built her a fine house when he turned to wheat
farming and cattle and never, as far as I knew, mentioned
where he found her.

I was happy for Nellie, of course, but I was jealous, too.
She had a normal life, a good man, children, her own
house. Just the things I would never have. I always
believed in making my own luck in business, and with
people. But this was one place my luck wasn't good. I
could see Richmond, love him and be loved. But I couldn't
be a normal wife, have children and leave The Life
behind.

1885

A fter the problems and crises of starting up the business, things sort of fell into a routine. I have no idea how many girls have stayed here with me, but they must run into the hundreds. Some I remember, some not. After a few years when the money was coming in steadily, I closed the house every August and went to French Lick or Hot Springs. I even got back in touch with my family. They thought I owned a store. They never came to Kansas City, but we would meet at some watering place for a vacation.

Since I owned the property myself, I didn't have to pay extortionary rents, although I spread enough money around the town. Everybody made money off prostitutes, with the girls making the least. There was the madam, the backers or landlord, the food merchants, the wine sellers and breweries, those who sold clothes, drugs and other things the girls bought.

Other than the customers I had known all along and who earned my respect, I wouldn't give a nickle for most of the johns. I had seen them at their worst and knew them for what they were.

But some wonderful people came into my life and that

kept me going—great girls, men anybody'd be proud to know and just ordinary people who were honest and straight.

The prostitute with a heart of gold was a myth some horny writer made up. But we were isolated in the resort, from poorer people and from respectable people and we formed a little family. We had our squabbles and jealousies and fights, but we looked after each other. If prostitutes have hearts of gold, it's for each other. Who else did we have? I've had girls who said I treated them better than their mothers. And others who wished me in hell.

Times were when groups chartered the house for a week or more. The great chain remained in place on the front door and the doorbell was muffled. There was no occasion to leave—we had food and plenty to drink, a barber, a valet, laundry, music and dancing. And girls.

Belle Waterman was one of my best girls for five years. She took a day off each week to visit her boy who lived with her sister not far from town. The rest of the time she read or sewed or played with a little pug dog. There were always dogs around the house. I wouldn't have had them myself, but the girls seemed to need something that didn't demand anything from them. They had quiet times during the day when they read or pressed their clothes. They didn't often go out, but when they did I insisted they dress in the very best, so I took them to John Taylor's or one of the other established drygoods stores, then found dressmakers to sew proper clothes. Then we'd rent a charabanc or hack and drive around on Sunday afternoons, showing off and seeing what was going on around town.

Belle left to marry a prominent man in town. No breath of scandal publicly attached to her and she seemed happy. She stayed away and I missed her, but I understood her position. She wrote me little notes and told me of all she did. But when her husband died, his people revived her past in an effort to deprive her of any share of his estate, which was considerable. They were successful.

When she came I said, "Belle, we can hire a good lawyer and fight them."

"No, it would bring scandal on his name. He treated me like a queen and I could never see his name dragged in the mud." She was resigned; I was mad.

"It'll be their name dragged, and serve them right, too."

"No, Miss Annie. I had a few years of happiness with him. Those years were more than I ever thought possible. I almost died here and I came back to life. Anything I have now is extra, more than I deserve."

"You deserve more than I can give you."

"It's enough." She leaned over and we embraced. She wore the quiet clothes of a proper matron and smelled faintly of violets.

"I took my boy back to my sister's," she said and smiled. "Now, may I have my old room back, or is somebody in it?"

I could not have come back so easily. I wondered at her equanimity and prayed that she would be happy. The first night, she drew a cherry boy. Billy Kearns' rapscallion uncle brought him and I gave him to Belle, knowing she would take care of him. Billy never stopped coming to my house over the years. He had a bland, smooth look and I always thought of him as the 15-year-old I sent upstairs with Belle.

She was as beautiful as ever, with a little more weight fleshing out her delicate figure. One day her sister and brother-in-law came and persuaded her to come and live with them and her son. I wondered if she could settle down after all she had gone through, but she retired from The Life and was content to keep house and live with them. She took what came and always made the best of it.

There were lots of other girls who married out of this house. Etta and Jennie entered the house so intoxicated they didn't know where they were until the next day. They worked here for a while and Etta met a wealthy man who came and spent a week. (This wasn't unusual; if the man could pay, he was welcome to stay.) At the end of the week he appeared in the parlor one afternoon and said he was ready to go, but that he was going to take Etta with him.

I didn't believe he was sincere but he convinced me and they left. I expected Etta to come creeping back in a few days, some the worse for her spree, but in an hour they were both back with a big certificate to prove they'd just been married by Judge White.

I wished her well as I always did the girls who married out of the house, but I never stopped feeling some envy. I had chosen The Life and was content with it, but I was sad that Richmond and I could never live together as man and wife.

Over the years, we met as we could. Richmond traveled for business; sometimes I was his business. We met in cities, at resorts. I usually vacationed at Hot Springs, Arkansas, or sometimes at French Lick, Indiana. Spas were popular and I enjoyed being at a place where I could be anonymous. Then several years passed. We made plans to meet, but a fire at the foundry prevented Richmond from coming. Another time one of his children and his wife were ill at the same time, probably with cholera. They recovered, but we missed another chance.

We wrote letters. They came and went at long intervals. We were both busy. His children grew. One was involved in a duel and was sent West. The girl married. The second son, the little golden-haired boy I had seen in his wife's arms that day, went to University, then began to read law. The baby, another boy, dismantled every clock and the pump, leaving a trail of unassembled parts behind him, but Richmond had faith this child would be his mainstay at the foundry. When motor cars and internal combustion engines came along, this child was able to move with the times, but that was later.

I read his letters over and over, trying to find between the words that lusty, youthful man I had known. The man who wrote the letters was distracted and weary, caught up in his routine which seemed ordinary to me, but called for all his energy.

The letters were written late at night, I sensed, when he was lonely. If he was faithful to his wife in the physical domain, he was adulterous in the emotional sense. He told me the worries he kept from her — the competition in his business affairs, financial problems. He told me how his children's unquestioning affection kept him from despair. His wife had ever been a saint of propriety, never lusty or intellectually curious or even very fond.

I wrote lively stories of what happened to my girls and customers. I asked for advice in business. I tried to let him know there was a fund of love he could draw on when he needed it.

We made plans to meet in St. Louis, but old Harlan died of a stroke in a girl's room, two girls quit and two took sick and I couldn't leave. Another time, the aftermath of the duel interfered, then his wife was so ill he was afraid to leave.

And so four years passed without a meeting.

By 1885 Hayes had come and gone and the bachelor, Cleveland, was president. The Statue of Liberty had arrived from France in pieces. The Brooklyn Bridge had opened. Women were pushing for suffrage. Buffalo Bill had started his Wild West show in Omaha and it toured the country with great success.

Closer to home, Jesse James had been killed in '82 in St. Joe. The Union Depot had opened in the bottoms and we survived a cyclone in '83. It took out two buildings in the next block, like a touch from the finger of God, but adjacent buildings were left standing. The cattle and beef business boomed and real estate ventures brought money to the town.

That summer, it must have been '85, I let everyone think I was going to Hot Springs and told only Ethel

Brandon, my housekeeper then, that I would be in a hotel on Michigan Avenue in Chicago.

I fussed as I packed new dresses, new face cream, new lingerie. On the train to Chicago I felt like a homing bird rushing to my meeting with Richmond. I waited at the hotel for word, afraid he would not or could not come.

I wondered if, in the years since he had walked into my bordello, the banked fire had died.

I refused to look at myself in the mirror for more than a glance. I didn't want to see the signs of age. I ignored the style of powdering to a dead white doll's face, so my complexion was healthy, but faint parentheses marked either side of my mouth. The chin, always determined, had taken a sharper edge. The chain of Venus lay more deeply in my neck. I was heavier. I could not read without spectacles.

Still, I forgot I appeared matronly. My heart beat as though I were twenty-two and unmarked by time, waiting for Richmond to come and begin to pull off his clothes and mine in an eager fury.

I was too edgy to sit still so I left the hotel to walk the canyons of the high buildings, look in show windows. It was too hot. Steamy wind blew heated gusts around the corners of buildings. The concrete city soaked up the heat during the day and I felt it through the souls of my shoes.

Would Richmond find me still desirable? I tried to prepare myself for changes in him. He might be bald, heavier, slower. But I could not imagine not wanting him.

I don't remember what I saw in the store windows. I do remember it was hot. It is always summer when I think about our meetings.

When I returned to my hotel he was seated on a heavy couch nearly hidden by a palm. The desk clerk directed my attention and I saw a cloud of cigar smoke, then a quick gesture as he rose. We nearly ran to each other, as eager as children.

"Annie." He held my hands.

"I'm here." I think if anyone had noticed us he would have thought us two silly fools, but I could see nothing but Richmond.

We went to the rooms I had taken and I ordered drinks and tea. We were awkward and slow, as we tried to become accustomed to each other. We overlapped each other's questions as we tried to tell all the events of the recent years all at once. We sat side by side on the couch in the hot room and looked out over the city, holding hands and talking, being close.

I stirred the hot air with a palm leaf fan. More air, just as hot, blew in the tall, narrow windows. A thin layer of grit had drifted in to mask the heavy tables and overstuffed chairs in the room where we sat. The windows of the bedroom adjoining were shut against the heat, the curtains drawn. It was weather for wicker chairs and lemonade outdoors, not dusty plush and dark mahogany in a city hotel.

Richmond had taken off his coat and loosened his collar before he sat, but when I ran my hand over his chest, he trapped it between the heat of his body and the heat of his hand. I was talked out, ready for love, but he held back.

"My wife has been very ill," he said. "I've worried about her. Then I've had to compensate for what she can't do. I didn't know the burdens she bore until I took them up myself." He gave a rueful half-laugh. I waited, trying to divine what this meant.

"I do love her, Annie." He looked at me to see displeasure.

"Of course you do," I said. I thought of all the people in my life and how each one brought out a different fondness.

"Nothing like us," he continued. "That was something rare." The word displeased him. "Rare. Not granted to many. When we came together, it was like a volcano. You were smart and fine—you knew it wouldn't last. You ended it. Did for me what I wouldn't do for myself."

Damp hairs stuck to my hot face. I drank some tepid tea. I waited.

"I did love her," he said. His hands now lay pressed on his thighs in a fierce stillness. "It is a calm love, thin and mild, but with affection. Consideration. Now that she is ill I feel I should have been kinder, should have done more."

"What more would she have let you give?" I asked.

He bent forward and buried his face in his hands.

I touched his shoulder and said, "I understand. And even if I don't, I accept what you are and love you."

"I'm not sure I can love you," he said in a croak. "It's been two years since I've touched a woman. I don't know."

I wanted to laugh. My randy imaginings would be for nothing. Serve me right. But not and can't are two different things. Although I knew every whore's trick, I would not do anything he did not ask for. Maybe it *was* can't.

"You don't have to do anything," I said.

"I dreamed of taking you down many times." He stopped and swallowed. "But I don't think I'm still a man."

I kissed him on the line where the brown of his neck was pale from his collar.

"Being here is enough."

"My wife has consumption."

Instead of pitying him or her, my spirit leapt with joy. Perhaps she would die soon and he and I could be together. I tried to hide both disappointment and elation. I shouldn't have thought such an evil thing—it would rebound on me.

"How long has she been ill?" I asked.

"Several years. She coughs and sweats, but tries to carry on. Sometimes the fever drains her and she can't get up from bed."

"That must be very hard on you."

He dropped his head again and I could feel the shudders. He had kept a tight rein on the sobs, which fought their way out. I took his head on my breast and comforted him until he stopped. I felt his tears soak through my bodice and I tried to absorb the shudders. He coughed and stopped after a few moments.

"You've held in a long time," I said.

"Yes." He blew his nose on a large handkerchief. "To save the children. They have their own grief over this."

I stroked his head. The thining hair revealed the delicate skull beneath.

"Let's be comfortable friends. You are the only man I have loved since I was twenty-two. I will love you, with sympathy, with care, with whatever I can bring."

I poured him a tot of brandy and he gulped it too fast, then choked. I pounded him on the back.

"That's better," I said. And it was. The color rose in his face and he smiled. I poured myself some tea and put my feet up.

"I had to come," he said.

"Of course. As did I."

"I want to take you to bed but I don't know what will happen."

"Whatever happens will be fine. It's ever so hot."

He reached over and stroked my bosom, then felt the stays beneath that propped them up. Then he patted his belly, which was also a little thicker.

"Take your clothes off, Annie. Be cool."

"The light is so bright in here. You'll be disappointed."

"Never." But he pulled the draperies and in the hot, dim light, I slowly removed each item. My skin was slick with sweat which ran down my sides and through my cleavage. The damp clothes piled up on the dresser.

I moved slowly. I knew I could make love — the demands for me were fewer. I was afraid I could no longer spark his desire, that age and time and worries had dampened my effect on him. I tried to smile, but I couldn't be lighthearted.

I could not watch his face.

I was barebreasted, down to drawers and hose. Without stays my midsection was soft. I bent to roll down my stockings and he rose and came toward me. I did not look up. He came up behind me and pressed himself against me, holding my waist so I wouldn't topple over.

I could feel his belly on my back, but even better, I could feel his member against my buttocks.

"I've risen to the occasion," he said, laughter in his voice.

"Lazarus from the dead?"

"Forget stockings," he said. He stripped out of clothes and joined me as I disentangled myself from my drawers.

He lowered himself on me and I took his weight in welcome. It was too quick for me, but I didn't care. I gave thanks to some erotic god.

"Didn't know you had it in you?" I teased.

"The old fellow came through."

"We'll have to give him some practice."

"I can think of a lot of exercises." Then Richmond laughed, a long, deep laugh that might have been buried as deeply as the tears. I giggled and tickled and teased.

Then he turned to me and made love — what he had forgotten in his haste, he now began. My nipples rose to his tongue and my own juices mingled with his. We loved each other with every touch of hand and mouth and at last, a slow gathering in my belly erupted and I arched away from the sheets, hips locked, legs rigid, hands grasping the headboard. I heard a groan that must have been mine and I collapsed, waves of shudders carrying me on. Then a touch alone would sent me off again and he laughed and held me through my spasms. Then he turned me on my side and entered again and we celebrated his resurrection. And Christmas and the Fourth of July.

We only went out for meals.

After a week on Michigan Avenue, we returned to our everyday lives.

Over the years I've burned hundreds of letters, lest they compromise someone. I didn't burn Richmond's, but they wore away from the touching.

Before I forget, there is the rest of the story of Etta. She wrote to me regularly. A couple of years after she left, she returned from the little town in Wyoming where she lived and said she wanted to room here for about three weeks and offered to pay me $25 a week.

"I don't want company," she said. "I'm not turning tricks. I just need a safe place to stay."

She had put on weight and looked prosperous and respectable with her trunk of stylish clothes. The leg-o-mutton sleeves and swirling skirts became her.

I thought nothing about giving her a room for a while. I though she just wanted some time to rest away from her home.

"I'm happy with my husband," she said. I believed she was true to him. At the end of three weeks she showed up with a baby about three weeks old.

"What's the idea, Etta?" I asked. "I thought you were happy. That isn't your baby. What are you trying to do?"

"I'm about to deceive my husband, but not the usual way," she said. She tried to keep from smiling. "He thinks I'm expecting. He wants a little girl and we don't seem to be able to have one. He didn't like the idea of adopting one, so I convinced him I had to come here to have this baby. I'm only doing it because I love him."

Etta stayed a few more weeks, then returned home and the baby passed successfully as her own child.

Time went by and she still wrote me. Later they had two boys of their own, but she said her husband thought more of the little girl "because she looked so much like her mother." She was a lucky little thing to have been found by such a clever and loving mother. Her daddy became mayor of their city and served two terms. The letters stopped about then, but I've always had the warmest memories of Etta and her deception.

Jennie, who arrived with her, eventually married a prosperous gambler who was awfully good to her.

Although Richmond was the only man I truly loved all of my life, I found loving friends over the years to fill the lonely times between our meetings.

Back when I was getting ready to build this house, I told Ned Stewart I didn't turn tricks. But he learned that I had special friends. Over the years I was friends with customers who'd been coming so long they were part of the scene and friends with men I came across running the business side of the resort. One I had known back in Kentucky, Ambrose Leary, was a buffalo runner. We were more loving friends and war veterans than lovers. Ambrose had his sprees in my house until he married. Tully McGee, a livestock broker, and I went to the Philadelphia Exposition together in 1876. I bought $35,000 worth of furnishings when we were East. He said he got more worn out buying things than he ever did driving cattle, which is what he had done before he became a broker.

Frank Greathouse was a special friend. He was born in the East and must have had a good education, judging by his genteel speech. For some reason he never told me, he went West and made his way after the War, first filling contracts for wood for the army at Ft. Riley, then hunting buffalo for their hides until that petered out about '76 or '77. He bossed cattle drives up the trails from Texas to Newton or Abilene. It was as though a prince had become a stable hand, but that was his way. He'd helped me through a bad time after the house first opened; I'd staked him a time or two when he was down on his luck.

I never knew when he would show up, but he always did. Then I'd put my housekeeper in charge, lock the doors to my suite and we would have a loving time, two old friends.

I always perked up when Frank came to town. I watched the girls in my house leave for better things and I was still alone. Of course, some girls went to the bad. I had to throw some out and I knew they ended up street walking or worse. But many girls became proper wives and mothers and built their own lives and I always wished secretly that I could quit and do the same with Richmond.

I suppose I could have sold out and retired, some time after 1880, but what would I do? There was nothing as interesting as being a madam. I was in The Life and it was my life and I didn't want it to stop.

But sometimes, when one of my old loving friends came to town, I thought about being alone and how it would be good to have someone with me. I could see myself growing old alone and I cried for the family I didn't have, then wiped my tears and said, so be it. If that's what life dishes out, I can take it. I've always taken what came and ended up on top. I can face anything. But there was a difference between knowing I was strong and liking it.

I wasn't really surprised when Frank showed up out of nowhere one night in a sweat. He asked to go to my rooms and waited until I locked the door, then pulled me away into a corner and said:

"Annie, I've a lot of money on me and there are three men following me to take it away. I want to leave it here in your care until tomorrow, when I hope to be able to make arrangements to move it to a bank."

I took his Stetson off and smoothed his hair back off his face. Once it had been the color of a sorrel pony, but now it was streaked with grey. He was broad shouldered, but had no hips to speak of. His face was brown and weathered, with squint-lines around his eyes. Years on horseback had bowed his legs and put heavy calluses on his big hands. He looked as though he'd come straight from the stockyards.

"Did you come by this honest?" I asked, half-kidding.

He gave me a look that said it was none of my business.

"Sit down and have a drink. In fact, why don't you just stay here. My man will screen anybody you don't want in."

"No, Annie. I don't want to enmesh you in this matter." He always spoke as properly as a schoolmaster. "I'm a cattleman, now, with my own spread. It took me three years of work and worry to make this money and no man is going to take it away from me."

Then from under his coat he drew a big bundle wrapped in cloth. It might have been a bundle of laundry, from its size, tied up in an old checkered tablecloth.

It wasn't the first time I'd held money. Men would blow in on the Santa Fe on a weekend with their pockets full of greenbacks from a claim in Colorado, or from a rise in the price of flint hides, or from selling cattle, as Frank had evidently done. I was used to obliging my customers, so this was just one more thing and I did have a good safe.

"In there," he told me "is $75,000."

"The stockyards aren't big enough to hold that many cattle."

"That was only the start of it. I sat in a poker game in a saloon on Liberty and won a couple of big pots."

"I don't believe you."

Without another word, Frank unknotted the corners of the bundle and there spilled out on the floor more money than I ever saw before or ever hope to see again.

I sat down all of a sudden and saw a grin fight its way

onto Frank's worried face. There was more than would fit into the safe, so I locked it up in a sewing cabinet in my bedroom.

"If you came by it honest, why are these three men following you?" I asked. By then he'd taken off his work coat and poured himself some cognac. He looked tired as he rubbed the scar on the bridge of his nose.

"You're going to devil the story out of me, aren't you?"

"If I can. You can't blame me for being curious." I pulled his boots off and put his feet in my lap and rubbed them while he talked. "Poker game down on Liberty Street?"

"I haven't been to bed since day before yesterday." He rubbed his nose again.

"Must've been a whale of a game."

"I didn't even get uptown or over by the depot to check into a hotel last night, just got those steers into the alley and walked into that poker game." He looked down at his dirty jeans and work shirt. "Played till this afternoon without even feeling tired. I won a lot of money and I wanted out before my luck turned. I was starting to flag, but these two men insisted I keep playing to give them a chance to win some back. When tried to leave, they got ugly. The third man stood by the door to make sure I stayed put.

"'I'm cashing in,' I said, along about suppertime. And I stood up.

"'No you aren't,' said the man who was dealing.

"'I just did,' I said and went to put on my coat. Then the one by the door said, 'You get by this first.' I was half-turned and saw him go for his gun out of the corner of my eye. He fired, then I fired. He barely missed me." He downed the last of the cognac.

"What about the guard?"

"I fired so wild it was a miracle I hit anything. He dropped his Colt and grabbed that arm. Must have winged him. I turned on the others and they kept their hands on the table. I bundled up the money in the tablecloth and backed out the door. 'First one out is dead.'"

"So now they're going to try and get their money back," I said.

"And get a bit of their own back, I'd guess. I thought I got away clean, but I saw them following me up from the Bottoms. I ditched them going in the front door of Maden's bar on Fifth and out the back way, but they're not going to stop looking."

He looked tired enough to drop so I said, "Stay here. My man will watch for them."

"I can't let them." He searched for words. "Hurt you or make any trouble for you."

"What are you going to do?"

"Go to the Pacific House and sleep until morning and hope they cool off by then." He lifted his feet from my lap and got up with a tired grunt and reached for his boots.

"I want to keep you here. Must you go? You always wanted to go to St. Louis. Let's get on the next train and just take off." I wrapped my arms around him from the back. "Don't go."

"Can't get you mixed up in this," he said and pulled away. It cost him a lot to say that, but I could read the care in his voice. He turned and ran his fingers down my cheek. It warmed me more than cognac.

"Careful doesn't say it." I helped him on with his coat and gave him a kiss. He took a better grip and kissed me back.

"That's until tomorrow," he said and managed a small grin.

I began to feel frightened as soon as Frank left. I could see three mean-looking men following him through the light, early winter snow that sifted over the city that night. The city was getting a little civilized, but men still wore sidearms and I could imagine the smell and smoke of a gunfight. I couldn't stop thinking of Frank's tired face and the gritting determination to do what he thought he must.

I imagined those men at every window.

Then I remembered that one of my girls had a friend, a petty thief, who would have torn the place down if he had known the money was there. He was a no good little snipe and I determined to get rid of the money before he did hear anything.

I slept poorly and was up earlier than my wont the next morning. I couldn't stand not knowing what happened to Frank. As a Texan might say, he wasn't much for talk, but he was right smart for doing.

A few minutes after nine that morning I went to the Pacific House, the best hotel in Kansas City then, to look for him.

I walked to the hotel in the snow with the sable collar on my coat turned up and my hands stuck into a matching muff. I looked as proper as any daytime matron when I approached the desk clerk. The lobby drowsed in the morning lull, the leather couches empty and the potted palms standing sentry, waiting for the evening's business. A waiter in the dining room moved from table to table checking place settings.

"Is Frank Greathouse registered here?" I asked.

"I'm sorry madam, but I cannot give you that information."

At first I thought, how tiresome, then I thought that Frank had been smart to have taken that precaution. I drew myself up to my full height and looked down my long nose at the clerk.

"I am a business associate. He failed to meet me this morning for an appointment. I must see him."

The clerk called his supervisor, Hans Gunter, who gave a start when he recognized me. More than once I had arranged for one of my prosperous gentlemen to be found dead in room at the Pacific, rather than in my house.

"Is Frank Greathouse in this hotel? If he is, which room is he in?"

"Oh, no, Miss Annie! Are you a friend of his? O Lordy, I wish't I'd known."

"What's happened?" I immediately imagined the worst, Frank dead and lying in some mortuary.

"We didn't know what to do," said Hans, who shrugged his shoulders, then rubbed his hands together and looked uncomfortable.

"What is it?" I asked, on the edge of panic. My heart pounded and I felt as though I were suffocating inside my winter coat.

"Come along," said Hans. "Room 315. Miss Annie, you're going to want to skin me alive, but hell, we did the best we could."

"Best you could what?" I fidgeted until the elevator reached the third floor, then followed Hans down the carpeted corridor. He unlocked the door.

I saw Frank on the bed—beaten almost beyond recognition.

I walked to the bed. His hair was matted with blood. One eye was swollen closed and the rest of his face was bruised and cut. I stopped the tears because I knew I had to stay calm. I pulled the counterpane back. His cuts had been cleaned and one arm was bandaged. Blue bruises just beginning to purple ran down one side and around his torso. His knees were scabbed over and his hands were cut over the knuckles, which were swollen and red. He was deathly pale and seemed to be barely breathing.

Pale winter sunlight shone through the high windows and the heat was tropical. I threw off my coat and knelt on the carpet by the bed.

"What happened?"

"We picked him up in the alley behind the hotel unconscious," said Hans. "Wouldn't have known who he was except for the key in his pocket. We got a doctor in. He cleaned up the worst of the cuts and filled him up with morphine."

"He nearly killed him with morphine." I was blazing mad at the doctor; there was nobody else to be mad at. It wasn't Hans' fault.

"Get some smelling salts and cold water." Hans started toward the door. "And black coffee." Hans flew out down the hall.

"Frank, Frank!" I didn't want to shake him because I didn't know how badly hurt he was. I laid my hand on his forehead, smoothing back his hair. He was clammy cold.

"Frank, wake up!"

I wrung out a towel in cold water and blotted his face. When Hans brought the smelling salts I tried them, then the cold water, then the salts. It took half an hour to bring Frank around.

"Frank, what happened? How did you get like this?"

"Annie?" He tried to focus his good eye, but he passed out again, then he roused himself. He was tough as an old saddle.

"What's going on?" he mumbled. His upper lip was split over the incisor.

"You didn't come back for your money." I didn't care a hang about the money, now, but I didn't know what to say.

"Annie, they took my poke."

"No, Frank. Don't you remember? You left it with me."

"Where's my money? Where's my money."

He'd been beaten almost to death and he was wanting his money. He started thrashing around and mumbling, then he tried to get out of bed. I caught him before he hit the floor.

"You stay here until I get back," I told Hans.

I went to the bank at Fifth and Main Streets, got hold of the cashier Holden, and asked him to meet me in Frank's room. Then I went back to my house, wrapped up the money and walked out with it under my arm.

Back at the Pacific House I went up to Frank's room. Before the banker and Frank, I spread out the money. Both counted it over three or four times and then Frank counted off five $100 bills and handed them to me. In those days that was known as a cartwheel.

"Miss Annie," said Holden, "anytime you want my bank you can have it."

One time, a few years later, I needed $1,000 in a hurry to send to my brother. Holden never questioned me, but wired the money immediately.

In the meantime, I took Frank to my house and we put him to bed in my room, swathed in one of the houseman's vast nightshirts. I knew it was hard for him to move around. I called in my own doctor who taped his ribs.

Frank lay white-lipped and still when the doctor finished. Grey stubble made him look seedy, but his color was coming back. After everyone cleared out, Frank said, "I don't know how to thank you for this, Annie."

"Don't. What're old friends for?" I leaned over and gave him a gentle kiss on the forehead. He automatically grabbed for my breasts dangling over him, then groaned when the pain stopped him.

"I feel terrible," he admitted.

"At least they didn't shoot you."

"Too many people about who would've heard a gunshot, I suspect."

"They tried to kill you elsewise."

"You should've seen what I did to them." He tried to smile, but his split lip made that impossible. I'd cleaned blood out of his hair. The tape held his ribs but he was covered with deep hurts and I wondered what was injured inside. He pissed blood for a few days, which scared me, but didn't bother him. I offered him laudanum so he could sleep, but he said my brandy was the best sleeping draught.

I wasn't in love with Frank, not the way I was in love with Richmond, but I loved his body. He was shorter than I by a few inches. I could trace the lines of the muscles in his arms through the flesh. His body stretched so wide at the shoulders that his coats wrinkled between the shoulder blades if he didn't have them tailored. A patch of reddish hair on his chest drew to a fine line running down the ridges of his belly to his pubic hair. His back delta'd to a small waist, then rose in tight little buttocks.

A few nights later, as we lay together in my big bed, I asked him why the money was so important. "You've lost a thousand on one poker hand and never blinked."

"The big ranches are making it harder and harder for little outfits to compete. I've spent three years getting my spread organized to the point where I can do more than break even. With this $75,000 I can be one of the big outfits. If prices hold and the grass holds and all the rest works out. I've got a wife to think of now."

I felt a cold stab. Why should it feel so bad? It was as though I were paralyzed through the solar plexus and couldn't breathe.

I got out of bed and pulled a wrapper over my gown. I got a drink of water, but I couldn't swallow. I left the tumbler on the washstand and walked over to the window. The weather had cleared and the light snow was melting back to the edges of the street and under lamp posts. I felt as though I had stopped, but everything went on as usual outside the window. Drays pulled their loads, people walked in and out of the shops on the next block. I could hear trolley bells and the shouts of the drivers, catch the smell of fresh droppings from the horse barn. It didn't seem right that the rest of the world didn't stop, too.

I tried to talk myself out of feeling bad. Frank and I were just friends; there had been no promises between us. I didn't see him for months at a time. But I couldn't do it. All I could think was, could I have married him? Did I miss my best chance? I had never thought of marrying anyone but Richmond, but now I thought I should have.

I thought about lying alone in the bed. Now it was tumbled, the sheets smelled of love and a man's sweat and my contentment. One day I would lie there, on smooth, silent sheets, with the smell of dust, alone.

Tears ran down my face and I didn't want to sniff and give myself away. I licked one stream that ran down and tried to make myself stop.

"What is it, Annie?" asked Frank. I heard him trying to get out of bed to join me, then he groaned and fell back. I wiped tears with the back of my hand and went to the bed.

"Congratulations," I said. I must have sounded strained. He took me in his arms as closely as his sore ribs permitted.

"Don't cry, Annie."

He didn't explain or excuse himself. He just held me and, of course, I cried even more. When I finally stopped and pulled a handkerchief out of the bedstand drawer, I said: "It just took me by surprise."

I felt empty and cold, even under the quilts. I guess I had thought that things would always go on as they had. I'd never thought how I'd feel about times changing. I'd thought about growing old alone, but I don't think I really believed it. That day it seemed as though it might happen.

Frank stayed until he healed up enough to go back to Texas. I sent a note to the police chief about the incident, thinking to save some other cattleman from that trio of thugs. I savored those days, thinking that when he got used to being married he might not come back.

1893

I would sleep alone in my big bed forever because Richmond's wife would not die. He found her the best care and she would not get better and she would not die. Her hold on him was strong the way lace is strong—it looks fragile, but knotted and twisted, it is stronger than woven cloth. She hung on year after year, growing more feeble, but never succumbing as her disease wasted everything but her will.

We wrote letters. We met several times at Hot Springs, Arkansas. Each time we came together like spark and tinder. It seemed absurd that such old lovers should hurry to bed like honeymooners, yet we did. We laughed and talked and strolled Bathhouse Row and ate too much. We got sunburned and I sat placid when he found some man with business interests to talk to.

Then there was a gap of two years some time in the early 1890s and when we met again I could see at once he was ill. The hawk's face was sharper, the skin drawn tightly over the bones. He was thinner and his collars ringed his neck loosely.

I wanted to cry and after a day of forced cheerfulness I did and told him what I feared.

It was always summer, this time in the brazen Arkansas heat, in a hillside hotel. A gentle wind pushed the curtains back and forth as moisture beaded a pitcher of lemonade. The rattan couch creaked with my weight as I rocked back and forth.

"It's nothing much," he said. "Just a little trouble with my pecker. Have to get up all hours and use the chamber pot."

"No, no, it's bad and you won't tell me." I could see the yellow cast to his skin and sense an off odor to his body. I knew and loved that body better than my own. Each time we met I had a new version of it, separated form the others in time, then gradually superimposed on the old.

"The doctor says it's just what happens to men when they get to be my age."

I stopped to calculate and was amazed that he must be near 65 or 66.

"We will never be together, except like this." I wept some more.

I was going through the change and while I had few of the usual problems to plague me, I did become upset easily. I was always healthy because I took care of myself.

He comforted me and I tried to spare him. He had to rest each afternoon. I lay beside him as he sank into a stuporous sleep. We tried to make love but the old ways did not work. That didn't bother me, now, but I was afraid it would distress him. But one night I said: "I can do things that would raise a corpse. I don't care if we couple or not—just to be with you is enough. But if you would like—for your own sake—I will do it."

He looked at me with a measuring glance. The baths and massages had left him drained instead of refreshed this meeting. A wicked glint lighted his eyes.

"Oh, you think you can."

"Surely. You do exactly as I tell you and I guarantee it."

He pulled me toward him and we tussled on the hotel bed whose springs sang each time we moved.

"You're woman enough as you are to stir the deadest desire," he said.

"Flattery," I said and nuzzled the greying hair of his chest. His ribs were beginning to show and loose skin drooped on his neck. I rolled him onto his stomach and began massaging him. I knew he did not want my whore's tricks. I wished I could pour life from my hands into him. I stroked and squeezed and kneaded and he relaxed. When I stopped he was asleep. I lay beside him sweat slick in the heat.

I got up after a while and pulled the curtains back. It was a heavy night, the air thick with moisture after a rain. A thousand lightning bugs flashed in the trees, thicker than I had ever seen them before. Miniature fireworks mounted as high as the tree tops, then the steady stars took over. The damp breeze blew through the room. I shivered despite the heat and knew this would be our last meeting. We had never lied to each other, but I granted him this lie, that he would not have to bear my grief with his. As soon as I had the thought I tried to push it away. But I knew.

We spent the rest of our meeting talking quietly on the veranda or walking slowly up and down the streets of the town. We made plans for the next meeting but after I returned to Kansas City there were no answers to my letters.

About six months later a small, flat box wrapped in brown paper arrived. A letter on his son's stationery, Phipps & Ballard, Attorneys at Law, lay on top.

"Dear Madam:"

"While going through my father's effects . . . "

Tears blurred the words of the letter and I couldn't see them. I took off my pince nez and tears rolled down my face in salty paths to my mouth. I sobbed and rocked on the chair where I sat on my desk. I had known this would come but it was no less painful when it did. I cried his name and wept for the time we never had together. I wept for all the ugly things I had said and done and wished forgiveness. I wept for myself.

It took some time before I stopped. I was cold and I stumbled to my room for a wrap. I didn't want to read the letter but I went back to my desk.

"While going through my father's effects, I found a sealed box with instructions to send this material to you and to burn the letters which were with it.

"My father died June 8, 1894, after a wasting illness of the kidneys. My mother had passed on the previous winter. In respect of his wishes, I am carrying out this duty.

"Your servant,"

"Clement Phipps"

I fumbled the string on the box, finally sawed through it with my scissors. Inside was a photograph of Richmond and me, taken in Chicago. There was a snapshot of me in a summer frock laughing under a huge leafy tree at some picnic, my face shaded by a broad-brimmed hat. There was a studio portrait of Richmond, taken before his illness, the wrinkles softened by careful retouching. There was a gold cigar case I had given him.

I began to weep again.

Three of my handkerchiefs lay on the bottom of the shallow box. They had been folded so my embroidered initials showed, but they had not been laundered. A faint trace of my scent still clung to them.

I grew old alone. Maybe it was just because I was going through the change, but I remember the time after Richmond died as one when I was melancholy. I hadn't even been able to attend his funeral and for some reason that bothered me. It was as though I would never be free of him, that he was still alive for me.

My girls kept me from going over the edge. They were

young and mostly cheerful and they noticed that I smiled rarely, so they tried to be gay. Nellie Darling was there, Ethel Brandon's successor as housekeeper. She kept me going. I did not like her unfortunate husband, but I did like her. Just having the house to run kept me going. There were customers, prosperous men without whom I would not have been able to operate. Molly Metlock opened her posh resort and gave me some competition. But there was no Richmond in whom I could confide.

Sometimes I wept. After we closed for the night, when everything was silent and dark, when the tiredness I had ignored crept up my legs and over my back, when there was no one stirring—then the sadness came and I wept to grow old alone.

I was an old walnut tree which bore no fruit, but nothing else grew beneath me. My strong branches and grasping roots pushed everything away except for flimsy violets and creeping pennyroyal. I could blame no one for the person I had become. I had made myself what I was—a strong, surviving, lonely woman.

The few days over the long years that I spent with Richmond are brighter in my memory than the ten years I spent with Billy Kearns. After the first rush of activity, Billy and I sank into a comfortable routine.

Nothing with Richmond was routine. There was always the spark waiting to ignite, the lust to be savored, the affection to be shared. Anticipation, then the release. I remember the dresses I wore, the rooms where we stayed, his body changing gradually with the years. I can remember the fringe on a bedlamp in Chicago, the taste of the water at Hot Springs, the texture of the skin on the nape of his neck. I can hear his voice in my mind's ear, speaking words that I still remember as clearly as the day he said them.

Richmond is an etching with each detail clear; Billy is a faded and out-of-focus Kodak, hard to recall.

I don't like to recall Billy Kearns at all, but he is part of my life and if I am remembering everything that happened to me, I must include him.

It was bad enough to lose my babes and husband when I was a girl. It was hard to give up Richmond when I was a bit older, but it was very hard to marry when I was much older, then have the tables turned on me. Perhaps it is because the early things happened so long ago and I've forgotten how bad I felt that Billy Kearns leaves me with a copper-bitter taste when I try to remember. If Richmond hadn't died, I would never have married Billy. As long as Richmond lived, I had hope.

I didn't love Billy with much passion. What is the difference? Sex is sex. With a whore, choices makes the difference. You must accept customers, but you may choose whom you love. With me, it was in my feeling. I was as good a wife as I could be to Willy Chambers and Billy Kearns, but my feeling for them wasn't strong. With Richmond, the feeling was overpowering, beyond my control. Sex with him became making love. We celebrated ourselves, marked the time of being together. It was the outward, physical thing that reflected our emotions. Sex for its own sake could be good, but making love was something beyond that.

I didn't care about Billy the way I cared about my babes. I gave him what was left of me to give—my sexuality, my brains, my humor. Of course, I gave money, too, but I could easily afford Billy. Perhaps if I had been wholeheartedly, holding nothing back, perhaps if I had been without cynicism, it might have been better. But there was always some reserve that I kept for myself and never gave to Billy.

Sometimes I think I held back because of the fear of appearing ridiculous. I was used to social isolation; I had heard all the names I was entitled to bear; I had no fear of what anyone could do to me; I'd faced the worst and come through. But I was afraid first that Billy was taking me for my money. Then I thought he was just taking me for a lark, to be able to brag he'd conquered the madam. But there was always the fear that he was taking me to show the world how obscene and ridiculous I was. I was over fifty when we married; an age when most women are grandmothers. I looked fifty—a good, healthy fifty, but no youngster. I suppose I further scandalized everyone who knew me, including the girls. Men married younger women, but women never married younger men. I had the money and the guts and the man—why not? Not many women could and of those women who could, almost none dared.

I think one of the reasons men in those days hated whores and madams was that we were independent. We ran our businesses and they depended on us. We made our way without having to marry or rely on fathers or brothers or husbands. I think marrying a younger man increased hard feelings in some quarters, but I never received any direct comment.

The money rolled in. Nellie Darling and I ran the house smoothly. I had made contact with my family in Kentucky and that summer I met two of my sisters in Hot Springs. We took the waters and talked and strolled. There were concerts and dances and musical evenings. I came back to the still-hot city in September feeling rested, but more than ever aware of the distance from other people. I never dropped the least hint to my family of my true profession to keep from shaming them and while I loved them, I always felt separated.

I don't know why Billy Kearns took a notion to court me. It might have been the instinct of a bird of prey which senses a helpless mouse hiding in the grass. It might have been the charity of a kind man reaching out to someone he felt needed him. When I am bitter, I think it is the first, but when it started my thought was: Here is someone who can make me laugh.

Billy had been coming to my house since he lost his

cherry. I can remember the night Belle Waterman took him upstairs, when he was fifteen. He was a gambler. Men who live by their wits with cards frequent sporting houses, even though most of the gambling went on elsewhere. Our hours coincided. Billy got in the habit of catching the last electric car and having a late supper with us.

He brought news from uptown, stories he'd heard. He would josh the girls and tease me and we'd have a few laughs together before he left for his rooms. He started asking me to become his mistress early on, but I laughed him off, thinking he was only looking for a free trick. Time went on and it was more and more of a habit to have him around.

The autumn lost the last of the color from the trees and grey winter crept in. The first big snowstorm caught Billy at my house. Once more he said I should let him stay. He had worn me down, like a cabinet-maker with a plane on a walnut board, until he'd smoothed away my objections and excuses.

"Let me sleep with you, Miss Annie. You wouldn't send a dog out on a night like this." Billy smiled and waited. I have to give him that, he was persistent.

"And if I do, will you expect it every night?"

"Let me try it once and I'll let you know."

"Oh, you don't think you'll like it?"

"I know I'll like it. You are the most beautiful woman in the place to me." He stroked my arm and looked expectantly at me.

"I'm twice the age of most of the girls," I said. "And what, about ten years older than you?"

"Time cannot wither your infinite variety," he said, mocking. "No, truly, you are a woman of resource and intelligence. They're ignorant chippies, pretty as they may be."

I looked at him straight. He was always carefully turned out and clean shaven in a day when most men wore whiskers. He ran his manicured hand around to loosen his stiff collar and I smelled a whisper of bay rum, then he reached toward my arm again. His blond hair was slicked in place and his skin was pink as a boy's although I reckoned he was in his middle thirties. There was always something boyish about Billy. Even his name was a boy's name. There was a softness to his round face that made him look young, as though he hadn't yet been in the world long enough for its experiences to mark him.

Here was a chance to have someone near me, at least for a while, someone reaching out to me. Could I afford to ignore him? This might ease the loneliness.

"All right, Billy." I stood and he stood, too. I took his hand and we went into my wine parlor for another drink.

"You don't know what this means to me, Miss Annie," he said when he took off his trousers.

"I don't know what it means to either of us, Billy."

I was afraid he would treat me with too much decorum, but once in bed, he treated me like a youngster. He joked and kidded and made me laugh. I moved muscles that hadn't been used for years. He talked dirty, like a foul-mouthed boy and I found myself responding as though I were a randy girl. I was surprised that my nipples still could rise to a touch, that the quickening moisture still flowed, that my body could still manage the filling and the crashing climax. Billy leaned over afterward and kissed me square on the mouth.

"That's the best ride I've ever had," he said and flopped over and fell asleep in a minute.

I lay awake wondering at what had happened. Thinking that this was an old pleasure I needn't deny myself. Thinking that Billy was fun and that I could use a little fun in my life.

The next morning I could feel the prodigies I'd accomplished the night before in my hips and knees and in my back. Parts of me that I used for loving were coming to life.

Things had changed by the time Billy and I got married in 1895. More people lived in towns and the size of Kansas City had more than doubled, spreading south and east from the old part of town where my house was.

President Cleveland married and brought his bride to Kansas City in '87. They stayed at the Coates House and opened the exposition building.

There was talk of a new city hall and courthouse and after years of talk, the boulevard system was being put in, designed properly by Kessler and others.

Then Harrison replaced Cleveland and William Jennings Bryan was making his name calling for free silver. The Ghost Dance War in the Dakotas had ended the Indians' hopes at Wounded Knee and the frontier was closed for most purposes. Some of my prosperous friends were hurt by the Panic of '93, but my business went on as ever.

We got married on June 4, just before my birthday. I was 52; he was 36. We picked up the license at the courthouse and found a minister to say the words. That night I gave a huge party for friends and customers.

Before the party I had my picture taken in the dress I wore that night. When the white brocade dress came special-ordered from New York, I had a local dressmaker embroider pearls into the pattern of the fabric. The full leg-o-mutton sleeves made me look heavy, but I must be in the current fashion. From the high, stiff collar to the little train, it was a dress for a queen.

Nelly Darling helped me arrange my hair that day, before I went to be photographed. She had packed the dress in layers of tissue and made sure my traveling case held combs and cosmetics. She braided my hair and pinned it into a coronet.

Nelly had been one of my girls before she met Murray. She had worked in another house, then left after they married. I didn't hear of her for a couple of years, but when my last housekeeper quit, she came asking if she could have the job. I knew her for a straight shooter, so I hired her. She had been the daintiest little thing, but years with Murray had worn her down. Her dark hair was streaked with grey and her figure had softened and thickened like a lump of butter in July.

"You're awfully quiet today," I said.

"Mmph."

"Something on your mind?"

"Not my place to say anything?" She smoothed tissue paper around my slippers and packed them in the corner of the box.

"Let's say it was. You're my good right hand. I need to know what's bothering you. We'll leave tomorrow and I want to know that all's well with you."

"I have a funny feeling about this Billy."

"So do I. What d'you think?"

"I think he's not to be trusted."

"Why?"

"Nothing in particular. Just the way he is."

"We got the wedding license. His intentions are honorable."

"Be that as it may."

I waited. She would take no more prodding.

"Should I call it off?" I asked.

"Not my place to say."

I didn't take offense. Truth was, I had doubts myself. I stopped at the florist shop for a bunch of roses on the way to the photographer. Somehow, it didn't look right cradling them in my arms and I ended up holding them down at my side to show off the dress. Looked severe in the photograph, as usual. In repose my mouth falls into a straight line and I knew I couldn't hold a false smile for the camera. My shoes pinched.

The day following the party Billy and I took the train to nearby Excelsior Springs where we strolled, took the waters and ate, then fell into bed as though we were the first couple on earth to discover love making. We stayed a week, then went back to my house.

If Billy was the black sheep of a good family because of gambling, the marriage shut him off completely. After the trip Billy went out every night, as regularly as he would if he were punching a clock. He was usually successful, especially at cards, but he'd bet on horse races, cockfights, dog races or anything else that came along.

"I hate to ask you, Annie," he said late one night as we sat over tea at one end of the long dining table.

"What is it, Billy?"

"I'm busted."

"What d'you mean?"

"I owe a man $3,000 from a horse race at the livestock fair and I don't have it."

"You can have it and no questions," I answered. "You always seem flush."

"Well, I'm like an actor. I have to put on a front if I'm going to make any money."

"I'll get it from the bank in the morning."

"Much obliged. Now, why don't we do something to take our minds off this subject, hmm?"

And so we did.

We settled down after a few months and started seeing each other for what we were. Billy would never quarrel, but he managed to josh me out of any complaint. He was a spank, one of those coddled children whose feet never touched the ground. He had that soft, fair, unmarked look of a child who expects the world to go his way, the child who was never spanked when he was little, even though he might have needed it. He had sneaky, soft ways and was plump for his height, like a naughty boy.

After that first time, he didn't hesitate to come to me for money for his betting. He seemed to think money was in the world for him to play with and he didn't worry about how much he had or where it came from. I had been tethered to the accounts book for so many years, I could never forget.

It was my pleasure to give him money and buy him clothes, pay his bills and be seen with him in public. There were those of his friends who accepted me and I remember our dinner parties and outings.

On one of those outings, we started early for a picnic in the country. Our rig rattled down Independence Avenue just as the congregation of an imposing church left after services. We stopped in the traffic and I saw Ned Stewart and his wife. There were three half-grown girls with them. I stared as much as I dared, to see what he had become. His sandy hair had thinned and gone grey. He was clean shaven, heavier and seemed to have permanent frown lines. The woman fussed over the girls who seemed impatient to be away.

Ned looked my way and I know he recognized me. He stared at me as though I were something in a museum — something interesting but dead and out of reach in the display case. Then he deliberately turned away without acknowledging me by so much as a flicker of his eyes.

I pretended I had some soot in my eye and turned in the seat so I couldn't see him even by accident. So that's what it has come to, I thought.

Seeing myself through Ned's eyes made me feel absurd. Across the street crowded with rigs I felt his scorn and it hurt not to be acknowledged by even a nod of his head. I distracted myself with the cheerful company in my carriage.

For Billy and me, the fiery sexuality that started our affair faded to weekly couplings when we came together like old comrades, respectful and appreciative of each other as we kept the bonds strong.

In the meantime, the new century arrived and The Life was changing. I didn't know what I could do to stop it.

All the Progressive ideas were to make life better, but the reforms didn't always have the results that people expected. For instance, they got laws passed that the factories in town couldn't work a girl for more than ten hours a day. Some had run twelve and fourteen hour shifts. What happened? They speeded up the machines to do twelve hours' work in ten.

The real push to wipe out the bordellos was not just the morality of the times but because women were learning to change and use laws to protect themselves. Men contracted social diseases in the low-class houses, then took them home and infected their wives. The wives must have thought that if there were no bawdy houses, adultery and disease would go away. But, like prohibition, the effect was different from what they expected.

Billy and I were in Hot Springs in 1909, talking about the European vacation later that year when we got word that a police order had closed the house. We rushed back to Kansas City and cancelled the trip. In the next several months I sought to induce the police commissioners to return to the old fine system of operation.

The prosperous men who had been my friends were aging and their power waned. Against the progressive forces, I doubt that even in their prime they could have prevailed. I learned that some of the policemen could be bribed and that, along with what 'pull' I had left, kept the business open.

One day Billy said to me: "You need to put your money somewhere safe. Invest in a business so that if the day comes when you have to close for good, you'll have an income."

"That's fancy banker talk from a man who only visits the bank in a casino," I said.

"I've got a chance to buy a business in Cincinnati — it does a good turnover — selling phonographs, electric pianos and the like."

I sat in my brown leather chair in my bedroom and listened while he dressed. "Those people we met at Hot Springs, weren't they in that business?"

"Yes, he's my contact. He told me how many units he sold a month, what the expenses were, how much he netted. Sounds like a good proposition."

"Sounds like you want to do it."

"I need $18,000 to buy into the business. I think this will be good for both of us."

I didn't like the idea. He had flirted more than I liked with the Cincinnati man's wife, if she *was* his wife, and it would mean we would be separated for long periods until he had the business going.

But he might be right. It might be good for us in the long run. The Society for the Prevention of Commercialized Vice was getting into high gear for another push and this would get Billy out of the way while I fought it. I needed no distractions.

"Let's go to the bank tomorrow," I said, "and establish a line of credit for you there."

"You won't be sorry, Annie." He gave me a quick peck on the cheek and went to his room to write letters.

Although I knew to the penny how much I had lent people, I never begrudged anyone and tried to be free-handed, but not foolish. I'd staked men before to starting-up money, so it wasn't just the money that bothered me about Billy. Sometimes I think a hidden part of your mind knows something that the open part tries to ignore. I've seen my hunches pay out often enough to trust them, but not wholly rely on them. I ignored my hunches about Billy and sent him off with good wishes. We had had more than ten years together and that's more than I had with any one man before. I stifled my doubts.

I first heard from Billy twice a week and his letters were full of the details of his new business. I didn't understand half of what he said, but it sounded good and he sounded happy. Then the letters trailed off to one a week, then one every two weeks, with less and less information in them. I had worries of my own, but I put together a traveling wardrobe and decided to go to Cincinnati. He told me to meet him at his place of business. Nelly helped me pack and we had another "Not my place to say" conversation.

I went straight to the showroom and was told by a pretty young woman there that he was out. I didn't know where he was living so I waited until he arrived.

He seemed happy to see me. He suggested I check into a hotel and we made plans to dine that night.

That evening the waiter cleared away the last of the plates and brought balloons of brandy.

"Business is not going as well as I expected." Billy said. He swirled the liquid in his glass and sniffed. Music from a string quartet played softly in the hotel dining room, where the sounds of silver on china and conversations rose from the tables.

I drank rich chickory coffee from a demitasse cup and said nothing, then offered: "You can always come back to Kansas City."

That was not what he wanted to hear. I suspected he wanted me to offer him another loan. But something had filtered into my mind.

"Why did you have me take rooms in this hotel?"

"No reason," he drawled. "My digs are a mess."

"Where are your digs?"

"Not too far from here."

"Are we going there?"

"I don't think that would be a good idea. I'll come upstairs to your room."

"I want to see your rooms."

"No."

"Because she's there."

He started and stared at me with a stupid expression of dismay. I hadn't known I knew until I said it, but I knew I was right and his expression confirmed my guess.

"Who is she?"

"She's related to the people from Cincinnati we met in Hot Springs." He sulked. "She has some pianos of her own stored at the display room and she was just looking after her own interests."

"Which included you?" Under the table I twisted my napkin.

He gave a simpering smile. "Just one of the things that happens," he said and shrugged. "Doesn't mean anything."

I wanted to tip the table of dishes into his lap. I wanted to scream and my throat ached with the effort of keeping my voice down.

"Just like marrying me?" My hands clawed at the linen in my lap. "I won't be treated this way."

He squirmed in his chair, his smile pasted in place.

"I'm writing you off as a bad investment, Billy. Good-bye."

I managed to stand without falling over the chair, then I threaded my way between the tables. I felt like a mechanical doll, legs jerky and awkward. I paused at the stairs, then picked up my skirts and climbed.

I left dinner in the bathroom sink and washed my face until it hurt, then had to rub cream on it. I was too mad to cry. It wasn't hurt-anger; it was disgust-anger. I was disgusted with myself for being so stupid about Billy.

I recalled the woman in the showroom who had spoken to me that morning. She was tall, with black, shiny ringlets which framed her face with soft tendrils. She had heavy-lidded blue eyes and a lazy smile I'd call kittenish, a way of teasing the person she looked at or talked to.

She was very young, perhaps twenty-five.

I was 62. I was still straight-backed and active, but my hair was white, my waist thick and the soft flesh of my upper arms swayed like turkey wattles when I raised them. I dressed well and felt healthy, but there was a second chin under the first. I was still a woman, but not a young woman.

The next I heard from him, he had sold the business and moved to Cleveland and the woman accompanied him. I divorced him as quickly as I could.

Nelly Darling and I were good friends. She propped me up when I got back from Cincinnati and told me some home truths to buck me up, as I unpacked.

"You never cared for him," she said. "Not like that man you used to meet." She re-folded shirtwaists and put them in my big dresser.

"No," I said, "but I was straight with Richmond."

"You always knew Billy was a little snipe, not to be trusted, but you let him jolly you into doing whatever he wanted."

"It was usually what I wanted."

"I thought I wanted Murray when I married Murray. He was a carefree man—the best dresser in the North End. I didn't know he'd turn into a drunk. Now I have to take care of him."

"You put up with a lot."

"He's my husband. His mistress is in a bottle."

"That's different," I said. I counted handkerchiefs before I put them away. "Besides, you still love him."

"Promise me, Miss Annie, if anything happens to me, you'll take care of him. He's not a bad man. He just has this weakness. He's agreeable until he gets too much to drink. I'd hate to think of him with nobody to look after him."

"I promise. But you're not sick or anything, are you?"

She shivered. "Felt a goose walk over my grave," she said and smiled thinly. "I just never want Murray to come to harm."

"I promise," I said.

I decided to replace all the draperies the next day and that occupied my thoughts for a while until I could think about Billy without getting angry. Then the upholstery had to be re-done to go with the draperies. In the meanwhile, the anti-vice people were pressuring Police Chief Hayes to close the bordellos as "public nuisances."

I always felt bitter about Billy in a way I never felt about Richmond or any other men I had known intimately. There was something about the way he did things at the end that left a bad taste. He wasn't forthright, like the others. But I think I always knew he was sneaky and I let him get by with it. He could lift the shadow of responsibilities from me with a joke or a smile or a trip to bed. And I relinquished my feelings to him and let him work me, first for happiness, then for bitterness. I try not to think about how I gave myself away and left myself open to his hurting. The last I heard, he was in California.

Remembering Billy makes me feel bitter and small. Lots of other things went on during those years. The city grew, my clientele grew, and the anti-vice movement grew.

It started when, as part of the Progressive movement, the idea of social hygiene came into popularity. People learned the true cause of syphilis and concluded prostitution spread it. The first push was to segregate the bawdy houses into a red-light district, such as New Orleans' Storyville and San Francisco's Barbary Coast or Baltimore's Block. This meant the police could control and regulate things while the houses remained open. In Kansas City we were segregated in the North End. When Eva Prince and Madam Lovejoy and Mable Heath and I established our houses we put them where people could easily reach them. As the city grew and spread southward, our resorts were left behind. The police station, city hall and other government buildings moved away from Market Square, business and hotels and theaters followed. We simply stayed where we were.

The world went on, the century turned and life changed. There was the war in Cuba and the opening of the Panama Canal, things we read about in the papers. The same movement for free silver and Grange and women's suffrage also brought about prohibition (1881 in Kansas) and all the rest of the progressive ideas. First the segregating, then closing the bawdy houses was part of the whole thing.

Theodore Roosevelt took over for the slain McKinley. Then Taft, then the slow steps toward war.

Kansas City grew, the Pendergasts' political power spread. And we celebrated the Priests of Pallas parade every year.

During all that time, at an age when most people think about taking it easy, I fought to keep going.

I should have quit, but I didn't want to rust away, alone, with nothing to do. When Richmond died, working was a way of keeping grief at bay. After I divorced Billy, it distracted me from hating him. Part of it was pure stubbornness. I'd not let the do-gooders, the police, the vice committee or anybody else tell me what I could do. Nobody had pushed me around since I had opened my own house and I wasn't about to let anyone start. Fighting back was all I had.

Along about then I had to stop having music because they could close me with anti-dance hall ordinances. Dance halls were where the seeds of moral corruption grew, so they thought. It was dreary without the piano. I had a Victrola, so couples could dance, and good food, but it didn't seem the same.

I had visits and letters from my old girls, which kept my spirits up. I kept one from "Ruby." I usually destroyed all letters so they couldn't compromise the writer, but Ruby only used that name in The Life and I kept the letter because it was honest.

Rudy was a rapscallion redhead who always had the house stirred up, what we used to call a stemwinder. She always was trying new hair styles, new dresses, new things with her tricks. She had her low times, but she was a bright light in the resort until she became ill and had to leave.

Dear Miss Annie (wrote Ruby):

No doubt you will be surprised to hear from me but I have been intending to write a long time and somehow never got around to it.

I've been home five years this month and it really does not seem that long but such is the case.

A friend of mine sent me the clipping from the K.C. Star about you . . . I could not help but cry when I read it. It brought back many memories—the picture of you as I first knew you and the inside of the house as well. It reminded me of the time twenty-three years ago that a half starved and half-clothed girl game to your door, ignorant in many ways and you took her in. You were a square-shooter and treated her white. That girl was me and while I was with you only a year, I have never forgotten you in all these years and so I am proud to know you and hope from the bottom of my heart, that you will have health and happiness until the end of the chapter.

You were not any "harder" than the women you had to deal with and so Miss Annie, I always remembered you with kindness and that is why I am writing to let you know how I feel.

As for myself, I have been on the square since I came home—never drunk and have never been in a night club. I stay home and keep house for Leland and my sister.

We have a nice comfortable home. Leland has the same job he has had for four years and never misses a day. My sister works. I do not have what I used to have but am content with the little I do have . . . .

You remember Fay Love? She has a fine position in Chicago. A friend of mine saw her there last summer. I am always glad to hear of anyone making good, and often wonder what ever happens to the ones who go on and on following up the same old game. You can't beat it.

I guess you know Lucille Oakland died two years ago. She had cancer of the stomach and died a horrible death.

She had very little left out of a small size fortune. Such is life.

Do you ever hear from Tempest? I would also like to have her address. Miss Annie, won't you have Murray write me. I would love to hear all about your selves.

Have to get busy and get my work done so will close. With best wishes, health and happiness, I am

Most sincerely,

"Ruby"

I had fond encouragement like that on one side and the Anti-Vice society hounding me on the other. The society got a law passed in 1913 that the brothels could be closed by permanent injunction as a public nuisance. I fought the law and continued to operate while the lawsuit worked its way through to the Missouri Supreme Court. But that didn't stop the reformers. They tried in 1915 and got the law through the House but not the Senate. They tried again in the 1917 and 1919 legislatures. All during that time I was repeatedly harassed.

One time, early on, policemen came to the house and demanded that we all go to the police station. They herded me and all of the girls into a horse-drawn Black Maria. The wagon smelled of piss and vomit and made me nauseated as we bounced against each other on the hard seats. The girls and I were properly dressed, of course. They murmured and wept, but I said: "I've called a lawyer. We'll get this straightened out." I was talking with more confidence than I felt. I could no longer ask Ned Stewart to represent me. He had stopped practising about 1902. This was a new attorney. He got the charges dismissed when he threatened them with some kind of writ.

Even though I was the Queen of Vice, I behaved with propriety in public and usually was treated correctly. But the policemen shoved the girls in and out of the wagon, called them "dirty legs" and generally did their best to humiliate them. They saw my grey hair and black-rimmed spectacles and they didn't try shoving me.

The old police station smelled of a thousand sins. My girls looked quite proper compared to a few drab street-walkers being taken to cells. The desk sergeant had the sense to look embarrassed.

"You ought to be ashamed of yourself, Matt," I said. He ducked his head. "I've paid you many a gift when you walked your beat by my house."

"There's a law against public nuisances," he replied, finally looking me in the eye. "We have every right to arrest everyone there." He'd filled out a little since the days I'd known him, shaved his handlebar mustache and taken on an air of responsibility.

"You didn't wait until we had customers. Why don't you run in the johns?"

"That's not necessary. The law says no bawdy houses."

"No, it doesn't," I shot back. "That case is still waiting for a decision from the courts. Until then, I have a perfect right to operate my business."

I could hear the doors of the cells slamming shut and the shouts of drunks. I could smell them, too. The scarred benches and desks and the scratched and battered walls were depressing. An old woman stood to one side trying to convince another officer that a neighbor had stolen her cat and burnt it in his trash barrel. The officer nodded patiently.

I didn't realize that first time what the lawsuit meant. They could come along and arrest all of us any time they wanted. True, the law wasn't decided, but they made trouble whenever they wished. They never took me to the station again. I always arranged the release of my girls; I never let one of them get sent to the municipal farm, although that was the aim of the arrests.

They never arrested any johns.

I made a proper effort to have my say. I have the clipping to prove it, from the *Journal-Post* of November 29, 1913.

In the meeting room at City Hall hard chairs stood in rows before the committee table. I knew that the committee members were successful businessmen, politicians and a minister—civic leaders. The only person who arrived before me was a newspaper reporter with his shorthand pad and pencil. A few other observers filtered in and took chairs and we waited for the committee.

I had prepared notes of what I wanted to say and I looked them over as I waited. I was a little nervous, but things had gotten to the point where I had nothing to lose by speaking out. I'd give that reporter something to take back.

In the news story he wrote: "A matronly appearing woman with white hair and spectacles and not at all flashily dressed appeared yesterday afternoon at a meeting of the Committee of the Society for the Prevention of Commercialized Vice.

(Did he think I'd come wearing a feather boa and spangles like some cheap chippie?)

He continued: "She sat down quietly and looked about her at a room full of men. When it became known that the woman was Mrs. William Kearns, better known as Annie Chambers, who had conducted a resort on the North Side for forty years, interest in her presence increased."

"I have a few things to say to the committee," I told Charles Sumner, who was the acting secretary, "but I prefer to wait until all are here."

I watched them buzz and flap amongst themselves, discussing my request. W. L. Eastlake, the chairman, conferred with the man next to him. Sumner, the secretary, shuffled papers and poured himself a glass of water. Another man arrived—a tall, lean specimen in clerical black—and they whispered amongst themselves, throwing glances toward me. Two more men arrived at the table. One smoothed his hair and the other checked his pocket watch. They all conferred, then the chairman shrugged. Eastlake gaveled the meeting open, then said: "You may have ten minutes, Miss Err . . . um . . . ah, but be brief."

I didn't think I could say everything I planned to say in ten minutes. Their interruptions made me repeat a little, but I thought I made my point.

"I think that the women should be put back where they were," I said. "If a smallpox epidemic breaks out in the city, you do not permit it to scatter, do you? No, you segregate it. But this vice movement has scattered these girls all over the city. Don't get the idea that I am speaking from a selfish standpoint. I am not. I am done, for I have been here forty years.

"These girls are in the main being thrown among the poorer class of people where children are growing up. Your movement has begun at the wrong end. Begin at the right end, and I will help you. Better the home surroundings, guard these office girls and others who are thrown among men to earn a living. Watch these cafes where little girls and young men go and drink of nights. Keep them from falling so that they won't have to go to a place of last resort.

"When they come to us they have no place to go. Their parents have turned against them, the church gives them no welcome, their friends spurn them and society kicks them further down. They are sick, heart broken and weary and tell us if we do not admit them it will be either the river or poison. We do not send for them. It is the haven of last resort when the whole world has cast them off."

I was nervous and spoke too fast at first. I was afraid they might cut me off after ten minutes. But once I had their attention I slowed down. They sat goggle-eyed now and I knew they'd hear me out.

"The girls in the houses in Kansas City did not come from here, but from other places," I continued. "But it was always the same story. The great majority of them had been working where they had been thrown among men in offices or stores, and their stories were most all alike. It was their employer, his son or someone with whom they worked who was responsible for their downfall. If there only was more chivalry among men there would be far less vice. The suggestion always comes from the man, never from the girl.

"Many of these girls have married good men who take them away from here and they have made good wives. This is the hope of every girl who goes there, and you'd be surprised to know how many of them do marry. And they marry men, too, men who know them and are willing to trust them. Ask former police chief Griffin how many of my girls were married during his administration. The department has the records to show for it. They are happy far away from here and have no desire to return. These girls will accept good men who will marry them and take them away."

I stood straight with my notes in my right hand while I steadied myself with the other on the back of a chair. The reporter scribbled away. I paused to make sure he was keeping up with me. My mouth was dry, but no one offered me a drink from the carafes on the committee's table. I cleared my throat. The room was high-ceilinged and drafty and smelled of earnest do-gooding government—sweat and dust, ink and old paper.

I told them how I had always contributed to church appeals, that I subscribed to local charities.

"Can you prove it?" asked Eastlake.

"In my files are letters which prove it," I said, "or I would be glad to let you see the cancelled checks bearing endorsements from the best churches in town."

That settled him down. He glowered and nodded for me to continue.

"The houses were taken off the fine list about four years ago," I said. "And what was the result: We had to pay about three times as much to grafters. It was a case of 'Pay me or I'll take you in.' It was a far worse condition than had existed before.

"Throw the mantle of protection about the young girl who has met her first fall," I continued, reverting to my original advice. "Why not help them when the time is ripe? You wait until too late if you expect to accomplish much by reforming girls who have had the public stamp placed on them by society. Don't begin at the place of last resort.

"I have been here forty years and I know whereof I speak. While I have helped many a girl rise where men had turned her down and her sisters had cast her off. Ask Colonel Greenman, who used to be humane agent, if I have not be instrumental in saving many a poor girl from this city. Our girls do not come from Kansas City, but from other places. Girls from here who have fallen go to the larger cities. They honestly seek work. Often they can't find it and if they do it is not a living wage and the result is the haven of last resort. But I never knew one who went there to stay and remain contented. They are human, just the same as others; they have hopes and aspirations which often are realized despite the lives they lead.

"Not long ago I wrote to the police commissioners asking to be placed back on the fine system. All the houses wanted it. I suggested that the money from fines be set aside and go toward the buying of land and the building of a real reformatory for women and girls. Not the old jail of a workhouse you have for them now. You have a nice place for the men, of course. Make a home for first offenders; keep them separate from the others and keep the negroes to themselves. Why shouldn't such money go toward reforming girls, the kind that are just at the threshold and susceptible of reformation?"

I told them that the result of the crusade was the placing of a ban on much valuable property through injunction which prevented the sale of it if one chose. "All insurance has been canceled," I said, "and thieves now run rife in the district carrying off all that is portable. The casting aside carelessly of but one match and all would be gone."

I said that ninety percent of the people of Kansas City favor segregation and that the majority of 3,500 women in one organization favor it. I had talked to a few people, but I was on shaky ground. I did want the do-gooders to know they might be anti-vice but they weren't necessarily the majority.

"There were twelve inmates in my house when the closing order came. Where are they now? Right here in Kansas City, but I'd cut my throat before I'd tell you just where. I have sent some money, but most of them are being cared for by good business men."

"To whom did you refer when you said that men held out their hands for graft money after the fine system ceased," asked Dr. G. P. Baity, interrupting my train of thought.

"I referred to policemen," I said without hesitating, "real policemen, in and out of uniform. That was the condition."

"You say these girls still are in Kansas City?" asked Julius Davidson, a member of the committee.

"Most of them are still here," I replied.

"Are they making a living?"

"Not the kind of living to which you refer. And not only the ones from my place, but from all the others."

"How are we to help them if we do not know where they are?" Davidson continued.

"You could not help them if you did. They would not accept a cent from this or any other organization. They'd die first."

The committee didn't have any more questions, so I went on and told of calling up a prominent citizen for one girl who desired to leave the city.

I impersonated the girl and told him that I wanted to leave the city and had a fine $60 sewing machine. He said to come and see him, and I sent the girl. He loaned her

$20 on the machine and gave her a ticket which read that if it were not redeemed in sixty days the machine was his. "Is that the way to help these girls?" I asked.

I had not paused because I was afraid the chairman would cut me off. It had taken more than ten minutes. When I did stop, I coughed and waited to see if anyone would say anything more, but my sewing machine story had shut them up.

I finished by saying that while we were on the fine system the women were not molested, nor was there trouble. Few, if any, complaints or robberies. I suggested a good place to begin the crusade of reformation for young girls would be the public parks, dance halls and cafes.

"I am awfully sorry that this thing has gotten into politics," were my parting words. According to the *Journal-Post*, the "astonished committee" did not get the full force of what I had said until I left the room.

I was downcast later when I read the reporter's final paragraph: "While admitting freely that the advice to 'begin at the beginning' was good and should be followed as far as possible, the committee did not take the rest of the talk seriously."

When I suggested they begin proper reformation for first offenders, I might as well have been speaking Sanskrit. What I knew for reality, they did not see. They had another version of reality which they imposed on the world which said that prostitution was immoral, that it would be good if it were wiped out. I wondered how they could ignore what I had seen for forty years—of girls treated shamefully and pushed into The Life by the rigid and narrow-minded "moral" people of the world. Prohibition could not stop people from drinking and closing the bordellos could not prevent people from having sex.

I've always believed in "Judge not lest ye be judged," and in my profession it pays to be broadminded. But the people whom circumstances, rather than virtue on their part, have put in comfortable and conventional surroundings judged those girls who weren't so fortunate. Proper middle-class women lived such sheltered lives, I couldn't fault them for ignorance, but the men who should have known better closed their eyes to what they could have done. Not punishment, but rehabilitation. Not patronizing me on Saturday night and listening to a sermon against "vice" on Sunday morning.

I never minded an honest con artist, but this has always been a two-faced town.

The house was padlocked in 1921 on an injunction proceeding brought by the police commissioners. We appealed to the state supreme court and won, so I opened the house again that year. But the law declaring bawdy houses a public nuisance had finally gotten passed in '21, and I was served with papers at the end of January, 1922. The filing date was February 28, 1922.

March 1922

Thathat day my new lawyer came over with the papers was a low day for me.

I had just come from General Hospital where my doctor had put me when I fell and broke my hip. My wheelchair was new, the caning fresh and white. My leg was out of the cast, but propped up on the adjustable leg of the chair. I was glad to have a regular dress on, but I had lost weight and looked as though I had shrunk inside it.

This attorney was a poor excuse, compared to Ned Stewart. Ned and I were friends as much as lawyer and client, at least at first. I remembered Ned's grin and the hair tumbling in his eyes when he was the age of this dour youngster. When Ned died I sent a wreath of roses anonymously, but I didn't try to attend the funeral. Any contact had long since been broken.

The youngster handed me the blue-covered legal sheets.

State of Missouri, Ex. Rel. Cameron   Plaintiff
L. Orr, Prosecuting Attorney of Jackson County, Missouri
vs.
Leannah Kearns, alias Annie Chambers   Defendant

They decided that I had "unlawfully established, kept, permitted and maintained" on my premises a "bawdy house, assignation house and place of prostitution: that said defendant was on said date using said premises and property and the furniture and equipment therein for the purpose of keeping and harboring lewd, immoral and lascivious women therein" and permitted "said women so harbored therein to receive and entertain men in the rooms" for "unlawful sexual intercourse, assignation, prostitution and for other immoral purposes and conduct" and that I was guilty of "establishing, keeping, permitting and maintaining a nuisance on said above described premises" and so on and so on three different ways around Jack Robinson's barn.

The injunction locked the doors and I was restrained from entering the premises or using them from March 13, 1922, to May 13, 1922. William E. Lyons, president of the Allen Investment Company was given permission to enter the premises to show it to buyers or lessees. There were none. Being closed down for two months wouldn't have put me out of business if I had continued to fight. But if I re-opened they could have come that night and slapped another injunction on me. It wasn't worth it. I had taken it to the supreme court in Missouri and won, but by then times had changed too much. Flappers were giving sex away and people thought bordellos were a thing of the past and good riddance.

Nelly Darling had died in the influenza epidemic right after the Great War, but her useless husband, Murray, stayed on doing odd jobs around the place.

After the lawyer left, I sat in the wine parlor with the legal papers on my lap. Financially, I was all right, but mentally and physically I had never been lower. I was too weary even for tears. The windows were cloudy and the cold February wind found its way around the sash. I must get someone to wash windows, the first nice day. Then I remembered: there was no reason for that anymore.

Murray went to answer a ring at the door, but I was too dispirited to move. Then he showed a man into my room. He looked familiar, the way everyone looks familiar, after eighty years of faces.

The man's hair was thin, going grey. He looked to be about sixty, a well-tailored business of some sort.

"Are you Annie Chambers?" he asked. I indicated where he could leave his hat and coat.

"Yes. What do you want?" I tried not to be brusque, but I was weary.

"You knew my father, Richmond Phipps."

My heart began pounding and I sat up straighter in the chair. I looked at him again for traces of his father's features.

"And you are?"

"Clement Phipps."

The son who became a lawyer and wrote me when Richmond died, mailed me the little box of mementoes.

"Please sit down. Won't you tell me why you've come?"

He pulled my desk chair over to where we could see each other. He looked around. Then he grinned and my heart felt light in my bosom. I could see Richmond in his smile and I smiled, too.

"I found my father's instructions after he died, so I carried them out to the extent that I mailed back that box of things. But I didn't burn the letters."

I felt confused.

"I read them," he continued. "They went back twenty years. He must have kept all of them. I suppose I shouldn't have read them, but I'm glad I did because I learned more about my father than I had known before."

"He was a wonderful man," I murmured. But I thought, that scallawag! To read my letters. And he probably knew me better than I wished.

"I promised myself I'd look you up. Today I've laid over on a trip to San Francisco to take depositions for a case."

I simply blinked at him, trying to understand. It had been close to thirty years since Richmond died.

"When I first succumbed to the temptation and read the letters, I was angry. I thought my father had been a moral paragon. There had never been a breath of scandal. He had cared for my mother through her illnesses with patience and affection. Those letters destroyed my picture of my father."

"If you stick your nose in where it's not invited, you'll find out things you don't want to know," I said. He smiled, lopsided, and nodded.

"Well, I put them aside and forgot about them. My family has scattered and my wife and I moved to a new house recently and I found them again in the packing. And read them again. Thirty years makes a lot of changes in a man's life."

Now it was my turn to nod.

"I came to ask if you would dine with me tonight." He looked at my leg. I felt like laughing, like dancing. But I said: "I'm afraid I can't go anywhere like this. But I will send my houseman out for something. I want to talk to you about your father." I instructed Murray to bring back dinner from a hotel restaurant uptown.

"You knew my father when I was a child," he said.

I paused to recollect. This mature man was the golden-haired baby in Mrs. Phipps' arms that day at the gate when she called me over. This was the child who reminded me of my own lost babes, fair and bright as the sunlight through his hair, the catalyst of my decision to leave Richmond. I felt a tear, then another and for once in my life, I wept without pain. The tears came without warning and coursed down my face and there was no sobbing nor heaving shoulders. I let them come and he waited. When they stopped, I wiped my face.

"Forgive me," I said. "The memories came back, a few at a time, until I overflowed with them."

"I didn't mean to upset you."

"Bless you, no. This is wonderful. Tell me about your father. I received letters, too, but I only saw him with my own eyes, never the way others saw him."

"Before I forget, I want to thank you."

I looked closely to see if he mocked me, but he seemed perfectly sincere.

"I want to thank you for making my father happy."

I smiled.

"At first I was appalled at my father's 'immorality.' Then when I found the letters again and re-read them I realized that you loved him very much."

"Yes."

"Those letters are so full of love that there could have been no harm."

"I never wanted to harm him. I left him once, but we found each other again."

"Whatever there was between you, I'm glad you made him happy. I always wanted to meet the woman who cared so much for my father."

I couldn't answer that. He didn't know what I had done for him, the child, that I had sent Richmond back to his family. Yet that day I was rewarded for the one virtuous thing I had done. He had come to see me and the love between Richmond and me was alive again because of him.

We had a drink together while Murray laid on supper, then he told me of the homely details of Richmond's life, his own boyhood memories. I learned how Richmond died and wept again, this time with pain. But I was eager to know all I could, pain or not. We talked all evening until both of us were empty and I thanked him over and over. Murray phoned for a cab and Clement waited in his coat. I pushed the chair to the door and we tried to think of one more thing to say. Then the cabbie honked outside.

That was really the end of The Life for me. The war and the attrition from the arrests made it clear that I could no longer stay in business. We won in court, but the law had me at last.

I opened my place as a men's rooming house during the twenties. When the weather was bad I told Murray to let all of the down and out men in. They'd help keep the burglars away. I never really recovered fully from the broken hip and although I could walk a little, I used my wheelchair more and more. My eyes got worse until I could scarcely tell dark from light.

After I heard David Bulkley's sermon over the whore's dead infant, I thought about my life and when a still exploded in the neighborhood, I met Mrs. Bulkley when we were all out in the street. She and I became friends and when they saw my reduced circumstances, they began taking care of me, bringing me meals and reading the Bible. No one believed I accepted Christianity in my old age and sometimes I think everything that went before happened to another person. Eva Prince forgave David back rent on her building which housed the City Union Mission and the Bulkleys were so kind I felt I could do nothing less handsome. I deeded this place over to them and in return they agreed to take care of me and provide for Murray should anything happen to me.

I was interviewed by A. B. MacDonald from the Kansas City *Star* in 1934 and there was a big open house at the Mission where I told the story of hearing David preach that sermon. It was focused and dramatic, but I was mighty tired of telling it before it was over. Then there was a surprise birthday party.

At first I thought they had forgotten a day that was important to me, in spite of several unsubtle hints. Maybe I've become childish. My birthday comes halfway through the year and balances the celebration at Christmas. Long ago I decided to celebrate it for myself, no matter what. Often there were no others to remember, although the girls always got me little gifts if they knew and we had our own party. I remembered things that happened by dating them from my birthday. I might not remember what age I celebrated, but I remember it was after a birthday that Belle Waterman took sick. Richmond died a few days after a birthday. The first reporter, Secrest from the *Journal-Post*, came around asking about my stories after my birthday two years ago. That was what started me thinking back over my life.

Beulah Bulkley, David's wife, came for me after dinner and pushed my wheelchair into the ballroom. As we rounded the corner, the lights came on and everybody sang "Happy Birthday."

Everybody came up to talk to me and there was the sound of conversation and laughter once again in the big room. Beulah brought me cake and a cup of punch in my own blue and gold china. I traced the edges and felt the delicate handle of the cup. I could hear the forks against the china and the clinking of ice in the punch bowl. After a bit, the Mission people sang and if the music wasn't as lively as it had once been, at least the sound filled the old room. People's footsteps whispered across the warped oak.

They told me they had replaced all the light bulbs so that the rooms were bright and that they had put up streamers and flowers all over the parlors. Some of my old girls sang songs, Stephen Foster, nothing racy, and everybody joined in. We remembered old times and I joked that it wasn't hard to trick an old blind woman, but I was glad they had.

The warmth of the people in the room seemed to warm me and once again I was surrounded by light and music and people enjoying themselves.

Before anyone left, I told them: "This is the best birthday I've ever had in all my ninety-two years."

After I became ill, I don't remember much. I told Beulah, "I want God to take me home."

I was so weary, so mortally tired that all I wanted to do

was go to sleep. There was a nurse. I remember seeing a woman in a white dress. Mostly, it was just dreams and the pain and the weariness.

One of my girls came to visit. She is a grandmother by now, but to me she was always a girl. We talked and I think she told a few other friends from the old days to come. Only the girls and Murray are left. All my prosperous men are gone. All the gaslights and long dresses are gone, all the music and dancing, all the sex and money and laughter.

My dreams played tricks on me. I awoke from a dream where I was a young woman again, full of vigor and health.

"There's my baby," I told the nurse. "See, he's smiling up at me."

Then I opened my eyes, but could see no more than when they were closed.

"Did you hear me?" I asked the nurse. "Pshaw, he would be an old man by now."

I remember his baby head, the sunlight glinting on the fair down, his skin warm and fresh. I remember burying him and wanting to die myself. I remember Willie's body when they brought him home, remember taking the ring off his cold finger.

I remember Richmond. I dream his body is still young and hard and I remember the drowning love. I remember the fire and the rings and our promises we couldn't keep, the meetings where it is always summer.

I remember Ambrose and Frank and Ned. I think of Billy with bitterness. I think of Belle and Big Mary and Etta and Nellie and all the girls and all the men, ghosts now. The walnut tree dies a branch at a time.

I remember Beulah's soft voice, and David, preaching God's love to those who would hear. I remember my conversion and the birthday party.

Then things begin slipping away and I can make no sense of it, and it is time to leave The Life.

Photo by Michael Andrews

THE AUTHOR

Lenore Carroll is the author of a traditional western novel, *Abduction From Ft. Union*, and some non-traditional short stories of the historical and modern West. She has taught Psychology and English Composition at colleges and a private day school since 1976. She lives in Kansas City, Missouri with her husband and sons. She is a member of Western Writers of America and the Kansas Posse of Westerners.